Sidney C Kendall

Among the Laurentians

A camping story

Sidney C Kendall

Among the Laurentians
A camping story

ISBN/EAN: 9783337424886

Printed in Europe, USA, Canada, Australia, Japan

Cover: Foto ©Andreas Hilbeck / pixelio.de

More available books at **www.hansebooks.com**

AMONG THE LAURENTIANS

A Camping Story

BY

SIDNEY C. KENDALL

TORONTO

WILLIAM BRIGGS, 78 & 80 KING STREET EAST

MONTREAL: C. W. COATES. HALIFAX: S. F. HUESTIS

1885

CONTENTS.

CAMPING SONG.

How dear to my heart is the silvery light
Of the moon, as she rises so gloriously bright,
As she hangs o'er the pine on the mountain's brow
And chases the gloom from the valley below,
And o'er the wild landscape her bright beams abound
Till rock, lake, and forest with glory are crowned.
In the stillness of night when the world is at rest,
Then Luna, enthroned on the mountain's crest,
Seems a guardian spirit, the long night keeping
Her watch o'er the earth while all nature is sleeping.
Oh! then to my soul is the scene of repose
A vision of peace for the world and its woes.

How dear to my heart is the quivering gleam
Of the water when kissed by her silvery beam,
When the light of the glittering wave is hung
On the edge of the shade by the pine tree flung,
When the woods on the shore grow dark and dim
With their sentinel shadows so tall and grim,
And the gloom of the forest seems dark and drear
By the side of the water so bright and clear,
On the lake's broad bosom the glimmering sheen
Like a halo of glory enhances the scene.
Oh! then to my soul is the scene of delight
A vision of beauty entrancing the sight.

How dear to my heart is a camp in the wood
When night has come down with her dark sable hood,
When the gleam of the fire-fly is seen in the shade,
And the glare of the torch lights the tent on the glade,
When the light of our camp-fire abroad is flung
Till our shadows are dancing the pine trees among;
As the glow of our camp-fire grows warm and bright
Our spirits rise high and our hearts grow light,
Our glad voices peal forth the jovial strain
Till the heart of the forest gives back the refrain.
Oh! then to my soul is the scene so sublime
That its memory lives through the rolling of time.

S. C. K.

AMONG THE LAURENTIANS.

CHAPTER I.

CONVEYS OUR PARTY TO THE NORTHERN LAKES.

HAPPY is the man whose soul is so in harmony with nature, that he finds his chief delight in forest and mountain, flood and field, and draws an unusual pleasure from the contemplation of not only the mightiest but the humblest works of God; such a man can never be really unhappy.

We claim that this love of nature is a possession by which most men are widely separated from their fellows. But let us not be misunderstood just here. We mean the faculty of finding pleasure in the very least of nature's gifts. The dullest and most obtuse of men will be impressed and awe-stricken at the

2

sight of the thundering Niagara, but not every one will appreciate the beauty of a mountain cascade or a forest rivulet. The most ignorant *habitant* will cower and tremble when the thunder booms above his head, or when the wild tornado sweeps across the plain, unroofing his barn and tearing up his trees; but from one year's end to another he would never notice the beauty of the morning breeze as it glides down from the mountain and curls the foamy billow on the sparkling lake. There is a beauty and a grandeur in nature that is not seen or felt by every one. To one man the virgin wilderness represents just so much lumber, or a covert for game: nothing more. Another, with bared head, will move among the stately pines saying in his heart, "These are Thy mighty works, Parent of good." His soul will be wrought with feelings akin to those that are experienced when he treads the aisles of some venerable cathedral; the silent forest is to him a temple not made with hands.

It is only our ardent love of nature that prompts us to pen these pages. So keen is our delight in the forest and flood, so full of interest are the memories of our sylvan joys, that even though these pages should never come to the public, we will endeavor to embalm them in the story of "Among the Laurentians."

We have not attempted a thrilling narrative of travel and adventure in foreign lands, but a plain, unvarnished account of the recreations of a party of students among the rocks and lakes of our own fair

Canada. We were sportsmen, of course, and by rod, gun, and the sweat of our brows we made our daily bread. Still, we were not hunters in the general sense of the term; that is to say, we had no designs on the massive denizens of our forests, and made no attempt to slaughter them. The stately moose and graceful deer were allowed to range the valley free at their own sweet wills. We did not aim so high; our intentions were more modest. There was not a man in all our company anxious to array his hall with the broad antlers of the moose, to exhibit to his friends as trophies of his prowess—purchased, forsooth, in some Hudson Bay Company's trading station. We were bound for the mountains of the north, on peaceable thoughts intent, anxious for nothing more than a few weeks' ruralizing among the lakes and hills, gathering strength and spirit sufficient to carry us through the next college term. Hence we were without the necessity of slaughtering any more game than was needed to sustain these mortal coils, so that our weapons were chiefly the fishing-rod and shot-gun, and, as a general thing, we made war on no bird, beast, or fish more ferocious than the savage pike or the fighting cock-partridge. As to the locality of our exploits, it will suffice to say the scene is pitched somewhere in the northern part of the province of Quebec, in the very heart of the Laurentian Hills, and nearly a hundred miles from civilization.

Now we must introduce the members of our party. This will not take long, as they are but four in num-

ber. The names we give them are only temporary,
and were enlisted to do service merely during the
campaign.

First. There is our worthy Captain, who is voted
to this post of honor by virtue of a great many
qualities. He is the son of a wealthy lumber mer-
chant, the owner of extensive limits in the region to
which we are bound. Being of a somewhat sportive
turn of mind, our Captain has spent a portion of each
year among the mountains, hence he knows the
country well, and has gathered a great deal of camping and sporting experience that will be of great service to us. The Captain, by virtue of his office and
position, provides all the camp requisites and sporting
accessories that we shall need; in addition to this, the
three sturdy bushrangers who will escort us into our
quarters are men in his employ. So by every right
and title he is appointed Captain of the expedition.

No. 2. This is a somewhat mysterious individual,
whose ways are past finding out. It was the verdict
of our college class for three years in succession that
we had no descriptive powers, and we never realized
the truth of that verdict so vividly as when dealing
with this very person. He is not a college student,
for he has completed his course, even to the extent of
going to Germany to put on the finishing touch, con-
sequently he must know more than any college
on this continent. He has a series of big capital
letters after his name that gives his signature the appearance of a well-furnished clothes line; yet he has

not adopted any profession, and we have no definite idea as to what he is aiming at. He is one of those grave and sedate individuals who are never ruffled, never excited, and, no matter how things go, never in the least disturbed. If he were an old acquaintance, like the next comer, we could turn him around before you, and trot him up and down to show off his points and peculiarities; but he is a stranger we have never met till to-day. There is something in his learned air and solemn bearing which led us in the first hour of our acquaintance to dub him Professor, and the title stuck to him till the end of the campaign.

Next! This is friend Zeno, though not by any means a stoic; a jovial, high-spirited medical student in the third year. If not the head of the party, friend Zeno is certainly the soul of it—a large-hearted, energetic fellow, who throws his whole soul, and body too, into work or play. And such an enthusiastic sportsman! just the kind of spirit for a comrade on an excursion like this.

No. 4. This is the tail of the expedition; an individual who may be described as a college student with a slight flavor of divinity about him. We have known this character for an odd five-and-twenty years, but he is still hard to understand and impossible to describe. He will figure on these pages as Nimrod, for the simple reason that he is not, and never was, a mighty hunter.

It is a glorious morning, about the middle of August; the sun is well on his way, but his power is tempered by a vigorous morning breeze, as we make our way through the streets of an old French town to the depot, where we meet with the Captain and his attendants, three hardy-looking Frenchmen, who have just arrived with our baggage on a waggon. Let us introduce them. Xavier—a dapper little fellow, who chatters like a magpie, and moves as though he were on springs, —is the cook of the regiment, and right well he understands his business. He speaks not a word of English, but enough French for six men.

Narcisse is the tallest and stoutest man in all our company; his shoulders and back are almost broad enough to tempt a bill-poster; a splendid fellow for the *portage* service; he will be able to carry both passengers and baggage at a pinch; and, another advantage, he has a good smattering of English.

The third is an ordinary style of Frenchman, with nothing remarkable about him, except his extreme taciturnity. He rejoices in the imperial cognomen of Nicholas, but when, for convenience' sake, this imposing appellation was familiarly abbreviated to Old Nick, a great deal of the dignity seemed to be lost.

Toot! Toot! is the signal for starting, and away we go.

This is not much of a train; there is only one passenger car, and that is a combination of first and second class. But we learn that this is an entirely new railway, and was only opened last summer; it runs about sixty miles back into the woods, and terminates at the end of the company's finances: that is to say, it is not yet completed, but will be carried farther along as soon as the directors are able to wheedle another bonus out of the Government.

There is a certain novelty about travelling on a railway of this kind : it is so different from the front lines, where everything is done in such a hurry and bustle. Here everything is carried on with an air of leisure that is quite unique, and the train saunters along from village to village at a sleepy rate of speed. There are no stations along this line, and the passengers get on and off with the most accommodating irregularity ; any old woman can bring the train to a standstill by brandishing an umbrella or waving a basket. There are no fences by the side of the road, · which necessitates the employment of an extra boy, whose duty it is to run ahead of the train and drive cattle off the track.

At last, when we have left the villages and clearings behind and are fairly in the woods, we bowl along at an increased rate of speed. The country now becomes very hilly and thickly wooded. We shoot through deep cuttings and over high embankments, along the edge of dizzy precipices and under overhanging cliffs, until at last there looms before us the broad river, and we have reached the end of the line. There is no station here, no hotel, no platform, no anything. So our baggage is all pitched unceremoniously out of the car and tumbled down the bank ; bags of biscuit, guns, tackle, fish baskets, etc., are all flung out, head over heels so to speak. The cars are unhitched and left *in*

statu quo, while the engine is laid up in a shed to
smoke his pipe and have a lazy time for the rest of
the day.

In the meantime we have collected all our traps at
the river side and are preparing to pursue our journey
by water. Our Captain has made all arrangements for
the conveyance of his party, so there will be very little
delay. Those arrangements, however, are worthy of
notice. The craft in which we are to proceed is a
large, flat-bottomed affair, about twelve feet long and
eight broad, which is expected to carry eight men,
a horse, and several hundredweight of miscellaneous
baggage. Every man will have to work his passage,
so we are each armed with a pike-pole to assist in
propelling the unwieldy craft.

Now, all's ready, every man to his place; cast loose
and away we go.

Hooking on to the slippery rocks, getting a grip on
the rocky bottom, and poling away with all our might,
we manage to make pretty good headway against the
current. This is certainly a very primitive and most
interesting mode of travel; it also affords a little of
the element of excitement to greenhorns, for an occasional slip comes near putting the amateur overboard,
and it is not long till even the Professor gets his dignity damped by coming down on his beam-ends on
the sloppy bottom of the punt. Some of us were
wondering what part the horse was to play in this
comedy, and now the enquiry is to be answered.
Yonder comes a narrow strip of sandy beach, reach-

ing as far up the river as we can see, forming an excellent tow-path. So the *cheval* is brought into active service, and we get a chance to sit down for a while and survey the scene.

We are among the mountains at last, without doubt, in the very heart of the Laurentians. On every hand they rear their verdure-crowned heads; so lofty are their beetling brows, and so precipitous their shaggy sides, that this broad river seems but a narrow stream between them. There is one right before us now, whose pine-covered crest seems to be dallying with the fleecy clouds that hover around it; the ledges and projections on his rugged front are fringed with groves of spruce and cedar, that appear at this distance to be mere sprays of moss and lichen. To such a majestic height towers this monarch of the hills, that we have to recline almost on our backs to glance along his shaggy front, up to the dizzy summit, as we glide slowly past his base. Many and various were the estimates given of the height of this particular cliff. The Captain's estimate, of course, was the highest; we shall not give it here, as we wish to retain some of our respect for Capes Trinity and Eternity. With the exception of a few short intervals, where we had to use the poles, we were towed gently along in this manner for about twenty-five miles, and about six in the evening we were deposited, bag and baggage, on the beach, within five miles of our destination. Our lusty porters were loaded first, to the utmost limit of their carrying capacity, and what remained we proceeded to distribute among ourselves. Xavier shipped a cargo quite out of proportion with his diminutive body, but he skipped off quite nimbly with his burden, although nothing of him was visible from the rear but his legs.

Near to where we landed were some small cabins, occupied by French-Canadian trappers, who gathered around us with offers of assistance.

Our Captain was now in his own territory ; for several miles around he was lord of man and beast ; so he had no difficulty in impressing as many as he needed for the conveyance of our goods. Among other favors, he secured the services of a sagacious dog, said to be an unusually good hunter. With this valuable addition to our forces, we shouldered our guns and plunged into the forest, on the trail of our bearers, who were already some distance ahead.

This is evidently not the virgin wilderness, for the best pines have been culled out, as we see by the stumps, four and five feet in diameter, which remain, though enough is left to make it a pretty thick bush. And this is perhaps a lumber road we are travelling ; it would be a passable road if its defects were covered with four feet of snow, tightly packed down, but now with all its projections exposed—well, it is a little better than a Quebec sidewalk, but not much.

As we advanced, the forest became more and more dense, and the deepening shades of evening added to this made it difficult for us to make our way as rapidly as we could wish, and we were considerably relieved at length to emerge into an extensive clearing,

in the centre of which there stood a shanty. It was
just light enough for us to see that a stream passed
through this clearing, which had been obstructed by a
beaver dam, forming a shallow lake, on the margin of
which stood the shanty we were in search of, to be
known henceforth as Camp Castle. We observed some
attempts at agriculture as we passed, potatoes, corn,
and other vegetables making some attempt to grow
among the blackened pine stumps. As we approached
the building we were greeted by the voices of our
bearers, who had arrived there before us; and also
by the savory odor of fried pork and onions. Our
genius of a cook, despite his big bundle, had made
such good speed that he had supper ready for us by
the time we arrived. Here we were to spend the
night and lay our plans for the future. This shanty,
with its stores of provisions, we were to use as a base
of operation and source of supply. It would also
serve as a place of refuge in case bad weather should
set in sooner than expected, and not a bad shelter
either, at a pinch, for the shanty was more comfortable and better furnished than the common run of
such places. It contained a large room furnished
with a stove, and bunks for a dozen, where our retainers proceeded to make themselves at home; also a
smaller room which we appropriated, furnished with a
table and benches, bunks for six, and a rack for firearms containing a small rifle and several fowling-
pieces. We had not time to pay much heed to our
surroundings, for supper was ready, and so were

we. How we revelled in fried pork and onions that
night! It must have been a most princely hog
whose carcase yielded those savory rashers. And the
onions! Even the Professor asked for more as ear-
nestly as any charity boy. Fortunately this was not
the first time Xavier had cooked for a party of sportsmen, or he would have been dismayed at the prospect
before him. We cannot speak so highly of the bed as
of the board of this establishment, for our cedar twigs
had been gathered in the remote past, and had been
slept on by several generations of sportsmen; so we
can declare they were not as "soft as downy pillows."
Besides we had friend Zeno for a bed-fellow, who
snorted like a whale and persisted in taking his half
out of both sides of the bed, leaving us the middle.
Still tired nature will assert her sway, and at length
we fell asleep.

CHAPTER II.

INTRODUCES US TO SPORTING LIFE.

BANG!

Hallo! What's that? That is a rap on the nose from coming rather violently into contact with the bunk overhead. But what was it that roused me so suddenly? Evidently the report of a gun; and now, being fairly aroused, I discover that my bed-fellow has departed. Glancing across the room I also observe that a gun is missing from the stand, and then it does not take long to arrive at an explanation of the mystery.

Brother Zeno has evidently appointed himself a foraging committee, and at the present moment is creating a mortality among the partridges. The rest of the household are still, to all appearance, sound asleep, snoring away as though they had to make up considerable lost time. No one seems to have noticed the report but myself, and while we are lying here at ease on our cedar twigs, there is friend Zeno out on the war-path hunting our breakfast. Now that I am awake it would not be a bad idea to join him in his labors and share his sport; so I crawl out of bed, intending to put the idea into practice forthwith.

The morning toilet out here in the bush is not a very elaborate affair, as we discard very little of our clothing for the night. So, after putting on coat, boots, and hat, I have only to girdle myself with a shot-belt, put a powder-flask into my pocket, select the lightest piece of ordnance from the rack, and step quietly out of the house, ready for action.

It is evidently very early, for it is scarcely daylight, and the morning star has not yet retired. The valley and creek are still shrouded in the mists of the night; around the margin of the lake, and along the winding passage of the water, only the tops of the spruce and cedars appear above the blue vapor, while the air is chilly enough to make one wish for an overcoat. Away to the east, above the forest-crowned hills, the horizon is glorious with the hues of dawn, and several shafts of light have glanced athwart the sky, heralding the advance of old Sol himself.

Yes, we have made an early start, and so much the better, for the day will be the longer, and the longest day will be short enough for the sport we have before us.

We made these observations at the same time we were making our way to the creek, for a second report informed us that our sporting friend was carrying on his operations in that direction, and as he has

with him our only dog, it will be necessary to join
him in order to share the services of that sagacious
animal. So we cross on the old beaver-dam and make
our way along the moss-covered rocks, skirting the
water's edge as closely as possible, climbing over
decaying logs and fallen trees, leaping from stone to
stone, and when that line of travel becomes too difficult, burrowing through the underbrush and making
short detours through the bush, but always using the
river as a base-line. All this time the only thought
in my mind was to join Zeno, and up till now I had
paid no attention to my surroundings. Suddenly,
from my very feet, up darted a big partridge, with a
whir-r and clatter that startled me, *pro tem.*, out of half
my wits. What an unlucky sportsman to lose game
like that from under my very nose! However, the
bird has not gone very far. We will follow in that
direction, and may get sight of it again.

Slowly, now, and softly, if you please. "With cat-
like step and stealthy tread," we are on the war-path,
and the consciousness of quarry, perhaps within gunshot, has aroused the sportsman. But the partridge
is a shy bird; we must respect his little peculiarities,
and approach him with becoming deference. If we
are going to have that bird in the stewkettle in time
for breakfast we will have to steal down upon him
like a lynx. So we advance with all possible caution,
stealthily, silently, not a leaf is disturbed, not a twig
is rustled, creeping, stealing, gliding, with our eyes all
over. Every tree, stump and bush is scanned from

top to bottom, until at last—can we believe our eyes ?
—there, on the limb of an old pine, not ten feet from
the ground, sits our prey. We are under the lee of as
fine a fat partridge as ever drummed on a log, not
twenty yards away, and in full sight. It is a sublime moment when we bring the death-dealing gun
to our shoulder and cover the devoted bird. Steady,
now ! It is five years since we fired a shot, and our
nerves are fairly quivering with excitement. But
surely at this distance it would be difficult to miss
such a splendid shot. However, to settle the question,
—bang ! and down he comes.

How that shot rang out clear and startling in the
still morning air ! How it rumbles and rolls among
the mountains, echoing from crag to crag as though
each separate peak were firing a salute to the king of
day.

But, in the meantime, there, on the moss with his
feet in the air, lies our partridge. It is almost with a
feeling of regret that we take him up and smooth his
ruffled plumage. Poor bird, cut off in his prime,
stricken down in the flower of his youth. A few
minutes ago we were quivering with exultation, but
now that the deed is done there really seems·very
little to exult over. There isn't much of the heroic
about it, after all, sneaking about in the woods like a
beggarly midnight assassin, stealing a march upon a
poor bird that is minding his own business, and blow-
ing out his brains from behind ; and there he lies on
his native moss, " with his own blood staining his own

fireside," so to speak. So this is what they call sport; it looks to me like a kind of murder. However, this is neither the time nor the place for sentiment, it is too near the hour of breakfast. Many a person who would moralize exactly as I have done would have no scruple about eating the poor bird if he were brought to the table. And here we are among the mountains, one hundred miles from the nearest provision store, and if we did not exercise our destructive propensities we would, in a few days, have nothing to eat; so we are compelled for the present to make a virtue of necessity, and, for the time being, become our own butchers. "Root, hog, or die," is the motto of the camp.

We are standing now on an elevated rock by the river, scanning the valley for some sign of our sporting friend. By this time it is broad daylight, the sun is evidently above the horizon, for the lofty peaks yonder have caught his earliest beams; but here in the valley it will be sometime yet before we are blessed by his cheering rays.

Here at last is the man I am seeking, making his way along the other side of the creek, with the dog at his heels, the gun on his arm, and, if I mistake not, a partridge or two in his left hand! He is evidently homeward bound.

"Well, friend Zeno, whatever induced you to forsake your virtuous couch at such an unseasonable hour of the day? Do you love to commune with nature; or were you attracted by the sylvan beauties of the—"

3

"Nothing of the kind," he replies, holding up a pair of partridges for my inspection; "I came out to get something for breakfast. I've no notion of ringing the changes on salt pork while there is any virtue in a shot-gun."

Zeno, you observe, is a thoroughly practical individual. There certainly is enough of the imaginative in his composition to make him an interesting companion at home or abroad; but this is completely overshadowed by the practical element; whatever he may be in theory, in practice he is a thorough-going utilitarian.

Perhaps it is as well for our physical comfort that this is the case, for the camp, after all, is a most practical place, especially when we are depending for subsistence upon the gun and rod. Your serious and meditative philosopher, who is able to draw moral lessons from all the petty details of rustic life, may be a charming member of our camp; but the man who can keep the pot boiling is indispensable.

Arriving in sight of Camp Castle, the smoke curling from the little chimney informed us that the garrison was stirring, and as we sauntered up the slope the Captain appeared, coatless, hatless, with his hair on end and his hands in his pockets, evidently just out of bed, and on his way to the brook to perform his ablutions.

"Good morning, Captain, rather chilly."

"Yes," was the rather gruff reply. "Cold as the—"

I did not catch that last word, but it sounded very

much like "chickens." Just here let me say, by way
of warning, our Captain, like most men of few words,
is generally more expressive than elegant in his remarks. This little hint will prevent any unpleasant
surprises in the future.

Seeing we have bagged some game, the Captain
graciously condescends to favor it with an inspection.
We have been out two hours and secured three birds.
To our great surprise we are now informed that if we
had gone to a certain place we might have bagged at
least three dozen. You will observe before long that
this kind of thing is another little peculiarity of the
Captain's. He evidently has great confidence in the
game-producing power of his hills, as well as the finny
populousness of his lakes, and is proportionately suspicious of any sportsmen whose success does not
seem to justify his confidence. Hence, no matter
what achievement we might succeed in accomplishing
with rod or gun, he was always ready with his narrative of some exploit that beat ours all hollow. I
would not like to say just what was the weight of the
big trout that was taken from the far lake last summer by some mythical personage; I only know that the
phantom of that unfortunate fish haunted our bright-
est days. Oh! but he is a facetious fellow, is the
Captain! and were it not for the sly humor that
twinkles in his eye during the spinning of those
yarns, we would have a poor opinion of our skill as a
sport.

Breakfast, gentlemen! That is a joyful sound

under any circumstances.   How much more so up
here in the mountains, especially to those of us who
for several hours have been bounding through the
forest, sniffing the aroma of the morning, getting up
an appetite as keen as a wolf, and preparing ourselves for an attack of the most galloping consumption.   It was an impressive sight as we filed into that
inner room and seated ourselves around the rough
pine-table, one at each point of the compass.   And
now, although a hundred miles from civilization, we
have not left behind all the refinements of life, for
there is actually a tablecloth ; true, it is only a copy of
the *Guardian*, which the Professor happened to have
in his pocket, but it answers the purpose just as well
as the finest of damask.   Xavier is rather jealous of
his reputation as a cook and waiter, so he hesitates
until we are all fairly seated, and everything in readiness, before he brings on the steaming dish, and—
here the curtain will have to fall.   If the salt pork of
yesterday were so delectable, the reader will understand why I shun the task of describing the fare of
to-day.   It will suffice to say, that whatever qualms
of conscience I may have had over the slaughter of
that partridge, they were all dispelled long before the
remains of the poor bird had disappeared.   I am prepared now to forgive any man who kills a partridge,
especially if he invite me to dinner, for it is my firm
conviction that they were made to be eaten.   During
breakfast a council of war was held relative to the
opening of the campaign, as a result of which it was

arranged that a detachment, composed of the Professor, Zeno and myself, should start immediately for Lake Clare, under the pilotage of Xavier, while the Captain and the other two Frenchmen remained to attend to some business connected with the shanty· We were to take with us the tent and provision for a couple of days, by which time the Captain agreed to join us with his companions at Lake Clare. After a few minutes' bustle we are ready to start. Our camp furnishings are all strapped upon the hardy little shoulders of Xavier, and the rest of us have only to carry each his own sporting accessories and blanket. The expedition is on foot. "Forward!" is the word, and away we go, single file, the Captain and his retainers waving us a farewell salute as our rear-guard disappears in the dense forest. The order of march is as follows : First : The dog, with tail erect and nose within half an inch of the ground, evidently smelling out the way lest we should run into the jaws of some ravenous beast. Next comes Xavier, playing the double part of pilot and pack-horse. Closely upon his heels follows brother Zeno, with his gun cocked and his finger on the trigger. He is doing his best to look both sides of the way at once, evidently on the look-out for something to pop at. Oh, the destructiveness of that man's nature ! Brother Zeno is for the present the commander-in-chief of this detachment.

Next in honorable order there strides the worthy Professor, our scientist and *savant*, who, in addition to his gun and rod, has armed himself with a formidable-looking double-barrelled spy-glass. Last, and content perhaps to be the least, there trails your humble servant, the historian of the campaign. By this time the sun is high in the heavens, the shadows have been dispelled, the whole valley is radiant with glory and musical with the varied voices of nature. There is a musical tingling of numerous cascades along the ravine, mingled with the soft rustle of the breeze through the pine tops. As an undertone to this, there is a low bass murmur which we recognize as the thunder of the wild Shewanegan, mellowed by the distance.

We speak of the silence and solitude of the wilderness. But there is no solitude to him whose soul is tuned in harmony with nature; no silence to him whose ear is quick to gather inspiration from the murmuring breeze or the rippling brook. I pity the individual who is lonely anywhere. Even here, in this desert wild, among these interminable forests and these everlasting hills, if there were not a being with whom to exchange a word, it seems to me that my soul would not be lonely; food for thought would be supplied by everything on which mine eye would rest, and by every sound which fell upon mine ears. There is a glory and grandeur in scenes like this that is not felt by every man. I am thankful for all the delight of social intercourse, and all the sacred joys of friendship that brighten earth's pathway and fill life with bliss. But in my heart I am also thankful for the strange delight, the almost unearthly rapture, which I experience in communing alone with nature and with nature's

God. One peculiarity of this wild region is worth mentioning, and that is the almost total absence of singing birds. Is it not strange that our feathered musicians should have such a partiality for the society of men that they are scarcely to be found beyond the borders of settled country? Can it be that the little choristers are conscious of the pleasure they impart, and, scorning to waste their sweetness on the desert air, prefer to trill their lays where they are best appreciated; or is their partiality for civilization to be accounted for by the fact that man is waging a war of extermination against every bird and beast of prey; so the sagacious creatures hover around our farms and villages, and repay us for their protection and sustenance by filling the summer air with melody. I am not attempting to explain the phenomenon, but simply stating the fact that the pine woods of the north are as bare of singing birds as Ireland is supposed to be of reptiles; and we hear nothing from the feathered population beyond the weird wail of the loon, the ghastly hoot of the owl, and an occasional scream from the eagle.

But all this time our detachment has been making good progress. We are now passing through a deep and narrow gully; rugged, moss-covered rocks are towering on either hand, in places almost meeting overhead; a sort of natural pass, but a very rough one under foot. Nature has been very accommodating in opening this passage through what would otherwise have been an unscalable cliff, and if the good dame had only

completed the job by laying down a good, smooth flag-
stone pavement she would have won our heartfelt
gratitude. As it is, there is a great deal to admire in
the remarkable chasm ; it is as weird and romantic a
locality as one would wish to see ; so shattered and
jagged are the towering walls that they are full of
cracks and openings, which here and there appear to
widen into considerable caves. Why, this place alone is
worth devoting a whole day to explore it thoroughly !
We might at least go slowly through it and take in its
beauties as we pass. Surely there is no need for such
unconscionable celerity, as though some deadly foe
were hovering upon our rear. Xavier is leading ; he
ought not to go so fast with that big bundle on his
back. Perhaps he would not if he had any choice in
the matter ; but that fellow Zeno is at his heels,
prodding him now and then with the muzzle of his
gun, and keeping up steam at the rate of five miles an
hour. Zeno is on the war-path, with blood in his eye,
so to speak ; his mind is on the trout, and with his
mental vision he sees nothing else ; every moment
with him is to be counted as lost until he buries a
hook in the maw of some hapless *poisson*. There is
the model sportsman for you ! What is romance or
the beauty of nature to him just now ? Less than
nothing, and vanity. Trout is the object in view ; and
these towering battlements, with all their rugged
grandeur, to him they are simply barriers to be passed
as soon as possible. And no insignificant barriers either,

especially those under our feet; for each individual rock is turned sharp edge up; and as they are covered with moss and slippery with last night's dew, the keeping of one's footing is a matter of considerable difficulty. At the present high rate of speed every step is attended with considerable danger to ankle, shin-bone, knee-cap, hip-joint, and every other part of our anatomy clear to the brain pan. But away with fear; are we not sportsmen, and game is ahead! So on we go, leaping, slipping, stumbling, and tripping at a rate which promises a rising market for court plaster.

Hallo! there at last is actually a place where the rocks meet overhead, forming a complete arch crowned with pine and veiled with herbage. Even our practical utilitarian commodore cannot pass that without an admiring glance, not he: it would not be in the nature of any man with a soul in his body of clay; so there is a halt for five minutes while we take in the novelty of the scene.

Never did these eyes rest on anything so unique. The arch is evidently caused by the ledges on one side sliding forward until the narrow chasm is completely roofed over for about twenty yards. No sunbeams ever find their way to the bottom of this ravine, and in the dim light that pervades the place every rock and crevice seems to start some wild suggestion. That dark aperture yonder at the base of that overhanging rock, what a splendid place for the den of

some wild beast; we can scarcely believe there is not
a bear in that gloomy recess, or at least a she wolf
with a litter of cubs. And, overhead, observe that
suspicious-looking ledge projecting just under the
cover of the arch. If there is not an eagle's nest on
that ledge there ought to be one; and if there is anywhere in the neighborhood a bachelor eagle on matri-
monial thoughts intent he could not do better than
secure his bride and take possession at once. There
are suggestive points to be taken in at every glance;
but it is not in our power to do justice to the scene,
especially as we have no descriptive powers. What a
sensation there will be, by and by, when some wandering artist shall ramble into this region with his cray-
ons or camera, and when the travelling public—the
pleasure-seeking, scenery-hunting public—learn something of the scenic resources of our own glorious
Canada.

"Forward!" is the word, and away we go on our
rocky march. A vigorous tramp of a few minutes, and
there at last is the blue sky right ahead.

But what has the blue sky to do down there in the
valley?

Why, that is the lake! To be sure, so it is, and we
are now at the water's edge. Nothing very remarkable about it with regard to size. A modest, unpre-
tentious little lake, lying peaceably in the arms of the
encircling hills. But a perfect little gem, fringed to
the very edge with emerald verdure, and reflecting

faultlessly as a mirror the few fleecy clouds that are floating across the blue heavens. Now, lest the reader should suppose we have come a long journey this morning, we will explain that the distance from Camp Castle to the shore of the lake is just one mile. But you know a man can see a great deal to think about in a mile of this country, if he only has a thinking machine on his shoulders.

CHAPTER III.

*FINDS US EXPLORING THE BOUNDARIES OF THE
BEAUTIFUL LAKE CLARE IN SEARCH
OF A LOCATION.*

WE have lost no time getting over that mile,
and it is quite a relief to lay down our
burdens and sit on the grass while Xavier
prepares for our further transport.   Out of
the rushes which fringe the margin of the lake he
draws a bark canoe, fortunately a good-sized one, but
not any too large to carry a party of four and all their
baggage.   After baling out the water, we pile our
things into it, and proceed to stow ourselves on board
as gingerly as possible, for the frail concern requires
very careful treatment.   Xavier, who is to supply the
propelling power, of course occupies the centre.   Brother Zeno deposits his burly form in the bow, bringing
the gunwale down to within an inch or two of the
water, the effect of which is neutralized by the Professor, myself, and the dog occupying the stern.

When all is ready, the shore recedes, and we glide
out through the rushes and water lilies on to the

clear, still bosom of the lake.   This is one of a chain
of lakes, of which Lake Clare is the fourth, so we have
some way to go yet by boat and portage before reach-
ing our destination.   Down at this depth, between the
hills, the morning breeze is not felt at all; and so quiet
is the water that the ripples in our wake are the only
movement visible on its surface, as the sinewy arms of
Xavier urge the heavily-laden canoe rapidly forward.

Brother Zeno cannot, of course, allow an opportunity
like this to pass, and immediately commences to unwind
his trolling line; but before he has got it fairly in the
water, the bow of the canoe is turned toward the bank,
and we enter a narrow channel, winding through the
woods, so hemmed in by trees that their branches are
brushing our faces, and so shallow that the canoe frequently grazes the bottom.

In a few minutes the creek widens, the water grows
deeper, and we emerge into the bright sunlight on
another lake, considerably larger than the one we have
just'left.   So clear is the still water that we can see
distinctly to the depth of several feet; and, startled by
the splash of the paddle, we discover fish darting off
in all directions.   This was too much for the irrepres-
sible sportsman in the stern.

"Arreté Xavier! this place is alive with fish; let us
have a cast."

"No, no, Monsieur! à Lac Clare! beaucoup de
poisson!"

So saying, the agile Frenchman plied the paddle
with redoubled vigor, and swept the canoe along at a

rate which effectually precluded all attempts to trap *les poisson.*

It was tantalizing, to be sure, but there was no help for it; Xavier had evidently taken his marching orders from the Captain, and was not prepared to receive any others until they had been carried out.

Another channel is passed, and we discover another and still larger lake, where, as before, our sudden appearance startles several good-sized fish, which were sunning themselves in the shallow water. This produces another appeal for a brief delay, and so great is our impatience that the Professor and I join in, and the effect of our united petition was to bring the Frenchman to a halt; not, however, with any intention of conceding our request, but simply that he might reason with us as to the advisability of proceeding without delay.

Crouching on the bottom of a shaky bark canoe is not a very favorable position for a display of oratory; but the Frenchman did pretty well. With gestures as energetic as he could venture to make without upsetting the tottering craft, and with a perfect torrent of French, the half of which we could not understand, he endeavored to impress upon us the necessity of making our way directly to our camping-ground, representing this wonderful Lake Clare as far surpassing any other lake known, or unknown, for the quantity and quality of its fish. And as for the ease with which they were captured, in the entire French language there was no word that was equal to the occasion ; so he met the emergency by a gesture as though he were filling the canoe with hay, and then, to settle the matter, he seized the paddle and literally churned the water with his vigorous strokes.

The Professor and I were laughing heartily at the Frenchman's eagerness. Zeno settled back with a growl of dissatisfaction, muttering that when he got to Lake Clare he would expect the fish to swarm around us, with tears in their eyes, begging to be caught.

In a few minutes we are landed on a rocky coast at the base of a lofty cliff, and as there is no water connection between this and Lake Clare we are to finish the journey on foot. The distance, however, is so short that we leave most of our things to be carried over by Xavier at his leisure, and, taking only our fishing gear, we start off in the direction pointed out. The trail leads us through another rocky gully, rising gradually to a level with the top of the cliff; the moss, in this instance, being worn off the stones by the tramp of more than one sporting party this very season. On leaving the gully we find ourselves in a dense pine wood, the tall, straight trunks of the trees standing like columns supporting the verdant roof; so thickly interwoven were the branches overhead that no trace of the blue sky was visible. So dense was the foliage that the gloom of twilight prevailed. It was the dim, religious light of the undesecrated sanctuary of nature. " This is the forest primeval"— it has never yet echoed the woodman's axe, and the

trees are standing where they have grown since creation's birthday.

Perfectly free from underbrush is this virgin wilderness ; far and wide the eye can range till the clustering trunks fill up the perspective. A few marks on
the trees guide us as we press on with eager steps
over the thick matting of fallen spines. In a little
while we begin to descend. The path grows steeper
at every step, and we frequently have to leap three or
four feet down ledges of rock. The pines become
thinner and smaller, underbrush makes its appearance,
and at length we emerge upon the sandy beach of as
charming a lake as these eyes ever gazed upon. This
is Lake Clare.

While we are waiting for Xavier let us take in the
scene. We are in the centre of a small, crescent-shaped
bay, with a sandy beach, about half a mile long,
bounded at either end by lofty rocks. Before us lies
a broad sheet of water sparkling in the sunlight.
Quite a breeze has sprung up, and the waves are rippling on the beach with a gentle murmuring sound;
while the overhanging birches on the bordering rocks,
as their long pendant branches are waving in the
wind, seem to toy caressingly with the dancing water.
On the opposite side of this lagoon rises a lofty cliff,
crested with verdure, presenting its broad, shaggy
front full to the glowing sunbeams. Whether this is
an island or the mainland we cannot yet determine.
Probably an island, for right and left of it the water
stretches away indefinitely, presenting long vistas

of the most romantic and picturesque scenery, with striking combinations of rock, forest, and water. In every direction the lake is studded with islands of varying sizes and forms, some of them barely appearing above the surface of the water; others rising a hundred feet and having their lofty summits crowned with pine and cedar. Some of them are grey, barren rocks; others are as green as emeralds with grass and bushes. Most of them rise precipitously from the water's edge, their borders presenting scarcely foothold enough for landing. The exceptions are where they have been overturned by some great convulsion of nature, and there they lie with the serrated edges of their stratified summits sharply defined against the clear blue sky. In the still bays and channels they are all faithfully reflected in the pellucid water that surrounds them. Altogether it was as fair a scene as one could wish, and yet only one of many in our fair Canada.

Here is Xavier with the canoe on his head! So, with a rattling of reels, a snapping of rods, and a whirling of lines, we are once more afloat and right into the business of the day. But before we can accomplish much there is another dispute to be settled.

The Professor is an adept with the rod and reel, and proposes that we proceed to one of the narrow channels and have a cast with the fly. But Brother Zeno, whose impulsive nature is ill adapted to such flimsy work, proposes trolling; and urges that we ought to

4

be moving about and exploring the lake. This last suggestion is unanswerable, so trolling wins.

Being the most expert canoeist of the party, I am. entrusted with the paddle, while the Professor sits in the bow calmly surveying the scene through his field-glass ; and Zeno reclines in the stern in a most comfortable posture, holding the line with his left hand, while his right hand shades his eyes, as he is peering in every direction, his broad countenance fairly beaming with delight, occasionally expressing his satisfaction in an explosion sufficient to scare all the fish within a mile. It is impossible to preserve any steady course, for he keeps me dodging about wherever he sees the least movement on the water. In one of these chases after a bubble he yells out :

"Hallo ! Nimrod. By the great hokey ! Take me down that channel. I declare to fortune I saw a fish as long as my leg."

Long before we can get there, the fish, if there ever were one, has departed for other scenes ; but Zeno must have the satisfaction of towing his hook wherever there was any indication of life. After a few minutes' peace he throws down the line and roars out :

"Say, Professor, old boy ! lend me that spyglass. If that is not an eagle on the top of that cliff yonder, I'm a Dutchman."

After a careful scrutiny of the object indicated, the Professor, with a sly twinkle, pronounces the eagle to be a wild goose. This rouses the ire of our ardent sportsman, who begs to be informed if he

hasn't any eyes, and assures us that he has lived long
enough in the country to know an eagle from a goose
as far as he could see it. And besides, he triumphantly
adds, whoever saw a wild goose perched on the top of
a cliff? The Professor, he declares, may be a master
of mathematics, but he evidently knows nothing of
ornithology, to call that a goose.

All through this little tirade the Professor has been
winking at me most immoderately; but of course this
was all side play, and was not visible to the wrathful
student in the stern. So after letting him vent his
displeasure in this way for some time, the Professor
hands over the glass, when the eagle resolves itself
into a projection of rock, about twenty-five feet in
length. Such is the delusive effect of the wonderfully
clear atmosphere and still water, that the cliff, which
is actually four miles away, seems scarcely one. So
for a couple of hours we glide about the glassy waters,
now skirting the margin of some lovely island, now
gliding under some overhanging precipice, now rustling
through a fringe of reeds which seemed to close the
prospect, and finding beyond a further sweep of glittering water stretching away between the islands,
until the eye lost itself in the tangled maze of rock
and forest; now darting swiftly across a broad lagoon,
or winding through some intricate passage, with the
branches of the overhanging trees brushing our faces.
Sometimes the rocky banks would seem to be hem-
ming us in, the water surface growing narrower, until
our progress is apparently obstructed by a lofty wall,

when an opening would be discovered barely six feet
in width, passing which, we would find ourselves in a
long, canal-like looking channel, the walls of which
were so straight and even that they seemed to be the
production of human skill, rather than the wild freaks
of nature. Along this canal we would make our way,
the gloom and chill intimating that the sunbeams
rarely found their way there; and then, most unex-
pectedly, we would emerge into the broad, clear, open
water. It was impossible to obtain any idea of the
form of the lake or the arrangement of its numerous
islands and promontories. It was a perfect watery
maze; a regular natural Venice. So confusing were
the sylvan passages and the heaped-up masses of rock,
that one wonders how a country so shattered and
jagged could hold water at all.

CHAPTER IV.

IN CAMP.

AVIER by this time has conveyed our goods across the portage, and stowed them on board a large, flat-bottomed boat which is kept on the lake. And after waiting some time for our return he decides to proceed to the camping-ground in hopes of falling in with us on the way, which is exactly what happens. So we drop into his wake and follow him for about half a mile, when he leaves us at a spot that has evidently been used quite recently by a sporting party. There are the ruins of their little stone fireplace; here are their tent-poles, and yonder stood their tent, as we can see by the layer of spruce twigs rolled flat by the weight of their weary bodies. Among the bushes we discover quite a heap of the *debris* of game and fish, which bodes well for our future comfort, as our commissariat is rather slenderly furnished; a bag of shanty biscuits, a few pounds of salt pork, a couple of tins of canned meat, tea, salt, and a few other groceries, make up the whole of it; our sporting skill must supply the rest. There is one comfort, however, the Captain with his contingent will be on hand in a day or two with fresh supplies from the shanty.

We have just about time to put up the tent and arrange matters before dinner. Indeed our appetites suggest that we dine first and work afterwards. But while Xavier is restoring the fireplace and frying some pork, the rest of us can be doing something. "So all hands to work; bring along the tent." And soon its white walls are glistening in the sunlight, while a diminutive Union Jack waves merrily from the ridge-pole. A dry recess is found under the cliff in which to stow our ammunition; it doesn't do to be fussing around a camp-fire with a powder-flask hanging to your waist. Near the same spot a stand is provided for our guns and fishing-tackle; there is no necessity to have loaded firearms standing around promiscuously, to fall down and send a charge of buckshot into some one's legs. A vigorous use of hatchet and jack-knife covers the floor of the tent a foot thick with cedar twigs; each man's blanket is rolled up at the head of his sleeping place; and we turn out to see how dinner is progressing.

Unfortunately we have not taken any game this morning; it would have been remarkable if we had, considering the noise we made and the speed we travelled. So there is nothing to do but to fall back upon the old diet. But it is surprising how palatable even salt pork may be, after such a morning's exercise in such a locality. Dinner is ready, and the attack commences. There is very little ceremony in the woods, so down we squat on the rocks and grass, stowing our legs away as best we can, some even stretching themselves at full length. We have no crockery, no table napkins, no cruet-stand, nothing but the bare sinews of war without any garnishing. Each man receives a tough shanty biscuit, about an inch thick, topped by a good-sized piece of fried pork, which constitutes his meal.

Grasping the biscuit firmly with both hands he hits it a bang on the heel of his boot, breaking it into several pieces, his jack-knife severs the pork into suitable portions, and so the meal proceeds. *Apropos* to this description will be the account of an incident which occurred during a journey on the Upper Ottawa. Quite a party of us were travelling together, and were driven by a storm of wind and rain to the shelter of a rocky island. It was too wet to make a fire, so we had to get up our muscle on biscuit alone. There was an old man in the party, whose teeth were so bad that he could not get along with the hard tack. However, necessity is the mother of invention. The rain had formed little pools of water on the uneven surface of the rock. Our aged friend placed his biscuit in one of these hollows, pounded it to pulp with a stick, and out of that primitive porridge-bowl, ate his meal with apparent relish. One must spend a few weeks in the backwoods to learn how few are the actual necessaries of life.

Dinner over, we take to the canoe once more and
spend several hours raking the surface of that lake
with every kind of hook and spoon that have as yet
been invented ; but concerning our success, it is only
necessary to say that we catch nothing—absolutely
nothing. We are as innocent of fish as we are of high
treason ; and, with every unsuccessful turn we make,
our disappointment and wrath increase until at last
we decide to give it up and go home to the camp to
have it out with Xavier.

Zeno declared it was the greatest imposition of the
nineteenth century. " To think of him dragging us
past those lakes alive with fish, to this place, where
there hasn't been a fish since the deluge ! A very fine
lake to look at, but that will be a poor satisfaction
when the pork gives out." So saying he advanced,
with indignant strides, in the direction of the camp.

The arch-impostor was lying, stretched at his ease,
on the grassy slope, with the blue smoke of his *tabac*
curling in picturesque wreaths about his head, while
the dog lay sleeping at his feet. On seeing us return
empty-handed an amused expression stole over his
countenance, which deepened into a grim smile as he
listened to our tale of woe ; and the only consolation
he had to offer was the opinion, expressed in the most
polite French, that we did not know how to fish.

This was adding insult to injury. For a man to
invest his money in an elegant forty-foot pole, all
aglitter with rattling reel and brass ferrules, besides
an extensive assortment of trolling tackle, and then to

be told that he does not know how to fish ; it was
more than human nature could bear. Our wrath was
considerably mollified when he condescended to explain that the finny denizens of this lake were somewhat different from all the rest of their species, and
require to be captured by a method peculiar to themselves.

This was satisfactory, although we had supposed that
we understood the habits of very nearly every fish
that existed in Canadian waters. Zeno, especially, is
heard wondering what kind of fish that can be that
he does not know how to catch. We shall probably
get some light on the matter very soon, for the Frenchman rises from the earth and promises to have some
fish for us in time for tea.

A flock of wild ducks had been visible all the afternoon, and now Zeno and the Professor take their
artillery and start off in the boat to have a pop at
them, leaving Xavier and I to try our skill once more
upon the trout.

I have been privately admonished to keep very close
to Xavier and observe him closely, to detect, if I can,
the art of capturing those mysterious fish ; and you
may be sure that not a movement of the wily Frenchman escapes my watchful eye.

We take our seats in the canoe and paddle swiftly
across the broad lagoon, threading a number of channels, till we reach a distant part of the lake, where we
pause, while my companion carefully scrutinizes our
surroundings to select the scene of operations. He

finally selects a broad channel running north and south between an island and the mainland. The sun is so far westward, and the cliffs on the island are high enough to throw a shade over the whole of the channel. Here I discover the first point to be observed. We had fished mainly in the sunlight, and without success; but our more experienced sportsman has selected a spot where the shade is so dense that the water is as dark as night. Now for the fish. I observe that he discards the large spoon with the flaring red tassel that we had been towing about all the afternoon, and puts on the smallest spoon we have, without any tassel at all. Next, to my surprise, he fastens on a piece of lead heavy enough to sink it to a considerable depth. Whoever heard of trolling with a sinker? The whole concern is then gently placed in the water; the canoe is put into rapid motion until about two hundred feet of line have been paid out; and then, with measured strokes, so gently and smoothly made that scarcely a ripple is left on the water, we glide silently and stealthily along.

I had been lying in the stern of the canoe taking in every movement and making a mental inventory of every part of the process, and I now began to see the philosophy of it all.

If so much caution and stealth were required, and such deep-laid schemes were needed, no wonder we had caught nothing. Now there was no ringing laughter to alarm the fish, no shadow of the canoe sweeping along, no splashing of the paddle. Xavier had discarded the new white paddle we had been using, and was wielding a small light one painted green, making his strokes so carefully and cautiously that not a sound was heard. The great spinning spoon that we had dragged along the top of the water, flashing in the sunlight, was more likely to scare the fish than attract them. Xavier observed that it might do for the pike in the next lake, but was useless for catching trout. Now there was a glittering speck deep down in the dark water that was likely to excite the curiosity of any trout within sight.

It is not long until there comes a tug at the line, and, simultaneously, a splash in the water about two hundred feet astern. Xavier quietly lays the paddle across the canoe and steadily draws in the line hand over hand. The prey is a trout weighing between three and four pounds. This is repeated several times during an hour and a half, until we have captured five glittering fish, weighing from one pound to three pounds and a half. Then, with the remark that this will do for supper, Xavier winds up his line and starts for home. Our friends have not yet returned, and, from an occasional report of their guns, we learn that they are still on the war-path. So we both go to work, Xavier to get supper ready, and I to collect a heap of wood for the evening fire.

Now it is time to give the reader a better idea of the situation of our camp. We have called the lake, with its numerous islands, a natural Venice, and, to carry out the analogy, the broad sheet of water in

front of our camp might be styled the Grand Canal,
for it was the broadest strip of open water in the
whole lake.   On the north side it was walled in by
an immense cliff, rising to the height of two hundred
feet, its summit fringed with spruce and cedar, while
its base was washed by the waves of the lake.   At
one point it fell back a considerable distance from the
water's edge, leaving a sloping plane, which was
covered by a grove of lofty pine trees.   This was the
spot we had chosen to be our temporary headquarters
during our sojourn in the wilderness.   Among the
straight, smooth stems of the pines could be seen the
white walls of our tent, while the smoke of our camp-
fire curled lazily upwards through the pine tops.

Right and left of us stretched the unscalable cliff,
while to the rear the ground sloped until it terminated
in a kind of ravine, down which there came pouring a
mountain rivulet, which furnished us with a plentiful
supply of cold, clear water.   So steep, and so close to
the water were the cliffs on either hand, that our
stronghold was only accessible by the lake; so that
when our boat and canoe were home, being the only
craft on the lake, we were entirely cut off from the
outer world.   It was as romantic and picturesque a
situation as can very well be imagined.   And then
our view in every direction fully harmonized with the
spirit of our surroundings.   But I have already dealt
very largely in description, and will not attempt anything further in that line.

Now the sun has gone down, the shadows are gathering on the face of the lake, and our friends have not yet put in their appearance. If they wait until dark they will have trouble to find their way back through this watery wilderness.

Xavier has been employing himself with knife and hatchet constructing a number of articles that will be both useful and necessary in our camp life. I have collected a good-sized heap of wood for the evening blaze, and now, as there seems to be nothing more to do till supper, we sit comparing notes of past experience until the last gleam of sunlight has faded from the sky and the gloom of the pine wood lies black on the water. And still they come not. It is evident by this time that they are lost. So, to give them a clue to our whereabouts, I take up a gun and send a shot ringing out into the still night air; but the report rattles and echoes among the crags in such a manner that it is a very uncertain guide as to direction. The flash might lead them home if they could but see it, but the report might as well be underground.

One hope remains: the bonfire. I will start a blaze that will illuminate the whole of the lake.

> " Ye stars, behind your veil of clouds retire,
>   For we will kindle on the earth this night,
>   To drown your rays, a cheerful fire."

Oh! the joy of a bonfire! Ever since I wore knicker-bockers, and burnt out my pockets with firecrackers on the fifth of November, my highest delight has been a roaring blaze; and there is considerable of the boy about me yet. A camp never seems to me to be complete until the fire is lighted. In a few seconds the pile is kindled, and, fed by the resinous gum of the pine, the flame leaps and roars, sending a ruddy gleam across the lagoon, and for a long distance around turning night into day.

"There, Xavier!" I shout triumphantly. "Clap on the frying-pan and kettle. That will bring them home in short order, and with hungry stomachs enough, I'll be bound."

I had scarcely uttered the words when a shout came pealing from the distance. At least I assumed it to be a shout; but really the echo of this region plays such pranks with every sound that a man can never be sure what he hears. But, by listening very attentively, I manage to distinguish the voices of our erratic comrades, roaring in unison, "Ahoy! ahoy!"

So, making a trumpet of my hands, I threw the whole strength of my lungs into a yell that would have scared a Mohawk, and really I was almost scared myself at the result. It is a novel effect to have your voice taken up by the invisible spirit of the hills and carried from crag to crag until you seem to hear yourself bellowing a mile away; and on a dark night it is certainly confusing, to say the least.

After this responsive exercise had been carried through a couple of bars I could distinctly hear the splash of oars and the rattle of row-locks, and soon the sparkle of water in the firelight told me that they were crossing the Grand Canal and would shortly be

with us. So, to give them a right royal welcome
home, I threw into the fire a quantity of pine gum
which I had in reserve for a supreme effort, and the
effect may be simply described as sublime. On they
came, through the fire-lit water, propelling the un-
wieldly craft with all their might, and singing "Home,
sweet home," slightly altered to suit the occasion. As
the boat grated on the beach, Xavier and I were there
to greet them.

"Welcome home, old boys; thought you were lost."

"So we were. We got in the rushes after those
wretched ducks, and didn't get out until after sundown; and we've rowed that miserable old tub miles
among those islands, until we decided that the lake
had no end to it. Why didn't you light that fire
sooner?"

"I wanted the fire for the night. But I fired a gun.
Did you not hear it?"

"Yes, we heard it; but it might as well have been
fired from the moon for all the good it did."

"Well, what about those ducks; have you got any?"

"Ducks!" roared Zeno in a wrathful tone; "don't
mention ducks to me for a month, if you value my
sanity."

"Why, how is this, Professor? You are a crack
shot."

The Professor shrugged his shoulders in an expressive manner, and replied: "Those are certainly the
most extraordinary ducks I ever saw."

"The ducks are bewitched," muttered Zeno, as he picked up his gun and started for the camp.

"What's for supper, Xavier? Did you get any fish?"

"Oui, Monsieur, beaucoup." And certainly the odor that mingled with the night air corroborated his statement.

Xavier's kitchen was an establishment by itself. He had been busy all day fitting it up to his liking, and preparing its furnishings in an ingenious though primitive style. The frying-pan was on the fire, filled with savory portions of fried fish; while on a dish of birch bark near by there was piled a fresh supply, ready to be cooked while the first spread was being dispatched.

"Well, you have been more successful than we have," remarked the Professor. "These are unmistakably trout."

As our friend Zeno came into the firelight the reason of his great discomfort became apparent. He was drenched to the skin, his clothes were covered with a thick coating of mud; and, as the night was very chilly, he was in a state that would have tried the patience of a much milder man. Evidently he must be dried and warmed before he will resume his accustomed good humour. Not having an extra suit of clothes nearer than the castle, he is under the necessity of extemporizing a costume out of the blankets; we arrange a couch for him, where his chilled body will get the benefit of the fire, seat ourselves right and left of him, and call upon our faithful attendant to " bring on the hash."

Xavier has manufactured some plates out of birch·bark, so we are now able to dine in a much more respectable manner; and, as fried trout is voted to be a grand improvement upon salt pork, we have no reason to be dissatisfied with the situation.

Xavier trots back and forth with fish, biscuit, and tea till every man is fully supplied; and then, heaving a log or two on the fire, goes back to the kitchen to prepare a second consignment.

He certainly will have to hurry about it: if one can judge by the flash of the jack-knives, and the vigorous working of three pairs of jaws, he will soon hear the cry of " Encore! encore!"

" Oh, but he is equal to the occasion!" " What a jewel of a cook!" " What a merry sizzle that frying-pan has!" " So soothing to the nerves of a hungry man!" " Was there ever anything so delectable as the aroma of that fried trout?" And in the same strain we might ask: Was there ever a more picturesque group than we presented on that occasion? Take in the whole scene, with the gloom of the forest for a background, the flashing, firelit surface of the lake for the foreground. The firelight playing on the straight, tall pines, the walls of the tent and the face of the cliff. For a centre piece, we three jovial mani-kins, two sitting cross-legged, the third lying at full length swathed in blankets, and all three munching away for dear life. Take in the whole scene and you

5

have a comical mixture of the sublime and the ridiculous.

Oh, but we had a glorious time that evening! How the fish and biscuit vanished it was difficult to describe. Xavier was kept as busy as though he were waiter in a first-class Parisian hotel; before his duties were over he had tramped quite a beaten path from the kitchen and back.

What merry peals of laughter broke the stillness of the night! What a stream of wit and humor flowed incessantly. Under the soothing influence of warmth, within and without, our friend in the blankets recovered his usual equanimity, and was able to take his part in the flow of conversation.

"After all, we have not done so badly for the first day," observes the Professor. "Partridge for breakfast, and trout for supper."

"And duck for breakfast to-morrow," I add maliciously.

"See here, young man, none of your sarcasm." This from Zeno.

"What about those ducks, Zeno? They must have led you quite a dance, judging by the mess you were in."

This inquiry led, of course, to an account of their afternoon's adventures, related by either of them alternately; and which resulted in much laughter on both sides.

"I am surprised that you did not bag a duck, though, Professor—a man of your skill as a shot."

"Oh, indeed! I had enough to do to act as guardian spirit to this wild youth. He would persist in following those ducks wherever they felt disposed to lead us, and I can assure you they led us into some queer places. But, to crown all, he got overboard into the mud, and it is a mercy he is not sticking there yet."

"How did that happen, Zeno?"

"It was in that vile bed of rushes. You see we could not use the oars, so I was standing up in the stern, poling the crazy old thing along, when I pulled myself into the mud."

"You mean you pulled yourself out of the mud?"

"No, I don't; so there is no blunder for you to grin at. The pole stuck fast, and the boat went on; and, as I did not know enough to let go, I found myself up to my eyes in the mud. I was never so near getting a dog's death in my life. Had not the Professor quickly backed up the boat and lifted me out by the hair of the head, this campaign would have come to a conclusion, so far as I am concerned."

It was rather serious that our first day should come so nearly closing with a tragedy, and a great cause for thankfulness that the calamity had been so timely averted.

The conversation became more serious as the time advanced; and our spirits reached a temper more in harmony with the spirit of our surroundings. The moon came up gloriously bright and clear, and invested the romantic scene with a new grandeur. Now, as the fire is getting low and we have used up all the wood

within reach, we decide to turn in for the night.
With the door of the tent closely drawn, and each
man rolled in his blanket on his bed of twigs, rock,
lake and forest, duck, partridge and trout are all
forgotten in that deep dreamless slumber which is
only born of health and weariness.

CHAPTER V.

SHOWS HOW WE AMUSED OURSELVES.

SUNRISE in the wilderness! To the contemplative mind of an ardent lover of nature, it is
one of the most interesting spectacles it is our
privilege to witness in this fair world. That
man is to be pitied whose sordid soul experiences no
thrill of pleasure, as he watches the gradual rout of
the shades of night before the advance of golden-hued
morn. But on the morning following the events narrated in the last chapter, the glories of the sunrise
were lost upon the little camp under the pines; for
there was no sign of life until the sun had been up
for several hours.

The first of the party to stir was Xavier, who
crawled out of his wigwam under the cliff, followed
by the dog who had been sharing his quarters. After
a few preliminary yawns and winks he proceeded to
light, first his pipe, and then the fire.

In the tent all was quiet as yet. We were sleeping
in a manner which was a strong recommendation for

cedar twigs as a cure for insomnia. I was very soon aroused by some one shaking the door of the tent, and the words, "Pardonnez, Monsieur." Looking up I discovered the brown visage of Xavier peering in. He muttered something which I interpreted to mean that this was a good time to be fishing.

"Do you hear that, Zeno?"

"Ducks be smothered," muttered that individual in his sleep, evidently with the events of yesterday fresh in his mind. The laugh I gave roused him entirely, and provoked the retort: "What are you giggling at so early in the morning?"

When the whole party was aroused I mentioned the fish, and related what I had learned yesterday concerning their capture. Among other things, that the fish were unusually active whenever any change had taken place on the surface of the water, either when it was first touched by the sunlight, or when the shadows of the cliffs began to broaden. So that, as Xavier had observed, this was a good time to be fishing.

But there was not a great deal of enthusiasm among us this morning; so Xavier was directed to open a can of meat, and leave the fish in peace for the present. In the meantime we would take a swim while breakfast was getting ready.

We were conveniently situated for bathing. We had only to disrobe in the tent and march *in puris naturis* to the water's edge, to paddle the boat out to about twenty feet of clear limpid water, and then jump overboard to kick, splash, dive, or swim, to our heart's content.

Oh, the delights of bathing! To crouch for a moment at the stern of the boat, with outstretched hands; to take the header and begone, like the vanished dream of youth.

Oh! there is joy in a vigorous plunge on a warm summer's day; to strike the water like a leaden plummet, and disappear with hardly a splash; then to emerge ten feet away, to dash the wet hair from one's eyes, and lay out with vigorous stroke at full length of arm and limb. There is life and health in a lusty swim, when the grasp of the limpid water feels like the embrace of an old familiar friend, and when the rippling wavelets lave one's cheek with a touch as gentle as a mother's kiss, as you breast the water, rising and falling with stroke after stroke; now on your side, with your arms thrown out in advance, churning the water like a small steam-tug; now on your back, with your hands on your hips and your face upturned to the blue sky; occasionally, in the sheer exuberance of delight, giving vent to a whoop which rouses the echoes and scares a flock of ducks a mile away. Keep it up till laboring lungs and weary limbs impel you back to the boat, when you find that you have scarcely strength left to climb on board. Oh, it is the very elixir of life! So we must have found it that morning; for the antics that were played by us three human porpoises would have been highly diverting had there been any spectators. After taking our fill

of watery joys, we returned to the beach and made a
hearty breakfast of corned-beef, biscuit, and tea.

Another long summer's day was at our disposal,
and amid the numerous joys of this paradise it remained for us to decide how the day should be spent.
There was one thing certain ; we had our living to get,
and whatever operation we select, it must be with a
view to the replenishing of our larder.

Before we had come to any conclusion, we heard
distinctly the sharp, clear crack of a gun, followed by
a rattling and rumbling among the hills that sounded
like thunder.

" That's the Captain's signal.   Hurrah ! Xavier."

Remembering there were three in the party, with
probably considerable baggage, we decided to take the
boat with all hands on board and give them a hearty
reception.

We had not expected them with us so soon ; but the
more the merrier, and perhaps our sporting attempts
will be the more successful under such an experienced guide as the Captain.

So we swing the old ark into the water with a
splash, scramble hastily on board, and away she goes
before a lusty tamarack breeze ; Zeno and Xavier
plying the sweeps, the Professor and myself pegging
away with the bow and stern paddles.

" Hurrah ! my merry boys.   Send her along."

" Allez ! Allez ! mes garçons," roars Xavier, and
accordingly she did go.   At every stroke her broad
bow strikes the water with a thump which scatters

the spray right and left, and threatens to stave in her crazy bottom. In a few minutes we land on the gravelly beach where the Captain and his party are awaiting our arrival.

"Hurrah, Captain! Hurrah! Narcisse, Nick'las. Welcome, all of you."

" But what a pile of baggage ; sakes alive, Captain, what are you going to do with all that ?"

There was just such an assortment of miscellaneous articles as a foraging party might collect in a successful raid on some lonely village. A bag of potatoes, a bag of biscuit, green corn, eggs, butter, a can of fat for frying ; cans of corned beef, salt pork, and a pair of chickens. Where in the world did he get them ? The Captain evidently hasn't much faith in our sporting skill. But it is possible that even game and fish would prove a monotonous diet without any change, so perhaps it is well to have a variety. Anyhow, heave them on board and let us get back.

By the time all our stores are shipped, and our little army of seven is embarked, we discover that the cranky old craft is afloat by a very small majority. She is so low in the water as to require very careful handling ; and besides, she leaks so badly in several places as to necessitate some pretty lively baling. However, she holds her own long enough to land us. in safety at our camp, and that is what is required.

" Well, Captain, what do you think of our choice of a situation ?" This was, of course, the first question after landing.

"Oh, it's the old ground; everybody puts up here!
Lawyer Blank and Judge Dash, of Montreal, hung out
here a month ago. It is a very good place for a camp,
but a poor place to fish."

Just what we expected to hear. And then, of course,
there came that old threadbare yarn about that sha-
dowy individual who pitched his tent in some unknown part of the lake, who got up one morning
when daylight was coming over the horizon; who cast
his line into the still water, just as the ripples were
kissed by the earliest sunbeams, and caught a fish
nearly as large as himself. But we had, by this time,
got accustomed to that old story, and reminded the
Captain that what we wanted was a good place for a
camp; as for the fish, we could very easily take the
canoe and go where they were. So the question of
location was settled *nem. dis.* It was then proposed
that we should proceed to the " Narrows," and try
the fly for the small trout.

The " Narrows " was a spot at the outlet of the
lake where the speckled trout were said to be abundant ; and, as the proposal was agreed to, we proceeded
thither at once.

Fly-fishing is the climax of the piscatorial art. It
holds the same relation to ordinary fishing that fine-
art painting holds to white-washing. Let no amateur
attempt to flourish the airy fly until he has honestly
worked his way up through all the lower branches of
his craft. But, after having angled and trolled until
the requisite quickness of sight, fineness of touch, and

delicacy of step are fully developed, then let him advance and try his skill with the hair line and gossamer.

Now he will discover some of the possibilities of the art. It is one thing to drag up fish by main force, flapping and struggling, from the bottom of the river; it is another thing to catch them on the wing, as it were, to entice them from their native element by an almost invisible line; and that is fly-fishing.

Given a fine clear day, just late enough in the season to be free from flies and mosquitoes, and there is scarcely any outdoor sport that will yield as much genuine pleasure as fly-fishing, if one is only sufficiently familiar with the art.

Imagine us, then, with a bran new rod, all aglitter and aglow, with a reel that works as freely as telegraph, making our way to the margin of the stream where the clustering birches cheat the sunbeams and make that deep shade which the trout love so well. Easily now; if ever you needed all the faculties of mind and body, this is the time. Line, fly, reel, everything is in good order; now advance with a step like velvet, an eye like a lynx, a muscle like a steel-trap, and an ear like a newspaper reporter. Don't get too near, the farther you can keep away the better; your shadow must not fall on the water. Let your imitation gadfly sail out with as natural a flight as possible; give it a few turns in the air, and drop it suddenly. Not a clumsy flop, dragging several inches of the line into the water but a neat fall, as though the

catastrophe had happened to the insect in the natural
course of events. Now let it drift about as though
blown by the wind; it seems actually to spin and
struggle as though alive; only for the line attached
we would be deceived ourselves. A little below that
last ripple there is a fish, if we mistake not, and
we will have that fish if we follow him to Je——rusa-
lem! There he is, hard and fast!

Ha! ha! my beauty, like many another fish, after a
life of dalliance, you are hooked at last. No use, my
gay deceiver, your career is ended; the best you can
do is to close it with *eclât*.

Skir-r-r-r! goes the reel; the cheeriest sound that
ever broke the stillness of a mountain stream. Away
goes our fish; give him the reel, or the line will snap
like a cobweb. But not too slack; hold him in check
and follow after. No need for stealth now, but skill
and coolness. Keep him out of those jagged rocks or
he is lost; give that snag a wide berth; now he is
resting, wind in the slack. There he goes again; give
him the reel. Skir-r-r-r! Never mind, you've got
three hundred feet of line, and he can take all he
wants. Don't get excited, it won't last long. Here's
your chance; run him into that land-locked bay, and
he will have scarcely water enough to splash in.
Cleverly done. Now he is yours. Lay him out on
the grass and make a mental estimate of his weight.

Such is fly-fishing, the prince of outdoor sports.

We had no great excitement on the present occasion
as our prey were all of a very small kind. We suc-

ceeded in landing a couple of dozen speckled trout, and might have taken a great many more, only that we would have had no use for them. We were not fishing for the mere purpose of destroying life, but only to supply our larder and keep the flame of life burning; and, when once our needs were met, we were not under the necessity to ruthlessly slaughter any of the creatures God has made. So, having taken what we considered sufficient for our present necessities, we gave ourselves up to the enjoyment of the romantic situation, without harassing either bird, beast, or fish. We tested the acoustic properties of a varied assortment of echoes. We explored a long chasm between two rocks which was dignified by the name of the Devil's Tunnel. We looked over a number of islands and took lessons in geology from their stratified borders. To crown all, we took another swim in the invitingly clear water. It was really difficult to keep out of that lake, so heated was the air and so enticing the water; so we were into it again.

We mention this matter particularly on account of a little excitement which occurred at the close.

I was the first to emerge from the glittering wave, and, dripping like a naiad, was proceeding, with tottering steps, over the rough rocks to where we had left our clothes. After a few preliminary shakes, I reached out for—the garment that goes on first; and, lifting it up, dislodged a big black snake that had coiled itself up on top of my clothes. Now, if there is anything in the universe I abominate, it is a snake. I abhor the whole race of them, from the Old Serpent down; and the unexpected sight of one so near me, almost in my hand, produced a most astonishing effect. I gave a howl of terror, leaped about six feet sideways, lit on a wet rock, and came down with a thump that made my teeth chatter. The Professor had just lifted his eyes above the water, after a dive, in time to witness my astonishing caper. He turned upon me a mild, wondering glance; but, at the same time, catching sight of the scaly reptile gliding down the rocks toward him, he uttered a shriek which was fully equal to mine, and threw himself into a posture of defence as though he expected to be attacked by an ichthyosaurus, or a crocodile, at the very least. The reptile took to the water with a readiness which showed it to be its native element, and went gliding along the coast with a wavy, sinuous motion, its hideous head just raised above the water, with its long, snaky body trailing after. By this time, having got my courage up to the sticking point, I seized a paddle and sprang in pursuit, calling out: " Come! Zeno, Captain, to the front—head him off!" Each man seized a club of some kind and gave chase. His snakeship was headed off into shallow water, and there we surrounded him. He made a brave fight for life; darting here and there, keeping us jumping about right and left, dealing out blows whenever he came within reach. Whack, smash, slap, splash went the clubs and sticks until the water was stirred up so that he was no longer visible. Then came an anxious time while we waited for his reap-

pearance. Imagining we felt his scaly body gliding
round our legs caused us to prance and caper in a most
energetic manner. At last he floated to the surface,
belly up, and was dragged ashore and found to
measure five feet long, and five inches in circum-
ference.

Zeno raised him on the blade of a paddle, and sent
him flying through the air about fifty yards into the
lake, to feed the fishes, and that was all the funeral
we gave him. Why we should have killed him at all
I can't imagine. But there seems to be in human
nature an unconquerable aversion to the whole serpent
species, and in some this aversion is so strong that the
very sight of a reptile produces a shuddering horror
which they cannot shake off. It would give us great
pleasure to exterminate the whole race of them, the
nasty, wriggling, crawling, slimy, scaly vermin!
Waugh!

CHAPTER VI.

DUCK-HUNTING EXTRAORDINARY.

E have given such a detailed account of our camp life thus far that by this time the reader will have a pretty good idea how we spent our time; and for the future we will confine our attention to matters of more than ordinary interest.

One of these matters, and not by any means the least interesting of them, was duck-hunting. A person may generally expect a reasonable amount of amusement when he goes in pursuit of the sportive duck, and our experience proved no exception to the rule. Our friend Zeno, after a somewhat brilliant career with the rod and fly, rapidly regained his ambition in the line of duck shooting. Day after day, as we roamed about the islands, those ducks could be distinctly seen, either flying through the air or diving and sporting on the surface of the water; and with all the glittering trophies he drew from the sparkling lake, poor Zeno refused to be comforted while the derisive quacking of those ducks resounded in his ears night and morning. He and the Captain tried their skill, and for a whole day pursued those long-suffering birds with relentless perseverance. They returned late in the evening, wet, muddy, tired and hungry, and, alas! to relate, never a duck to show for their trouble. The Captain explained their want of success by the fact that the ducks had been so repeatedly fired at that it was impossible to get within range of them, for they were as wild as hawks. Zeno was rather gratified than otherwise, as the breakdown of such an old sport as the Captain tended rather to clear his own reputation in the matter of the previous failure.

Matters were getting serious; and it was unanimously agreed that the time had come to strike a decisive blow for the honor of the camp.

We held a council of war that evening by the light of the pine knot, and the conclusion we came to was that we should advance the entire line for a general attack. Accordingly, word was passed to Xavier to be on foot at first peep of dawn and have a day's rations put up. We saw very little of Narcisse and Old Nick, they being absent most of the time on business for their employer. It subsequently transpired that they had been engaged on some secret service in our interest, the nature of which will be revealed hereafter.

Next morning the whole garrison was astir bright and early. There was a grand filling of powder flasks and shot belts, and looking up of artillery in preparation for a general *coup de etat.*

6

It was not much more than broad daylight when we embarked; each man carrying ammunition and provisions for the day. The cliffs on every hand were lighted up with the dawning beams; but the chilly mists of night still hovered around the islands, as we proceeded slowly to the seat of action, taking with us both the boat and canoe in order to be prepared for any emergency. Arrived in the vicinity of the ducks, the flotilla was quietly moored by the side of an island, while the Captain and I ascended to the top of the rocks to take in the situation and formulate some plan of procedure. The sun by this time was high enough to light up that part of the lake we wished to explore, a brief survey of which revealed the reason of our previous failure. The ducks had chosen their lair with a penetration which showed very plainly that they were up to the dark ways of man. It was a long, broad field of water, entirely surrounded by beds of rushes, and so formed that we would no sooner enter the field than we would be at once perceived. The banks of this lagoon were formed of soft mud, so there was no possibility of attacking them by land. There was nothing to do but to advance boldly in, when the ducks would immediately retreat, keeping just out of gunshot; if hard pressed they would take to the rushes or glide down one of those side channels into another pond, and by the time we could sight them again they would be rushing back into the lagoon. This kind of wild-goose chase might be kept up all day, or, for that matter, for a whole week, without the slightest chance of success; the Captain was aware of all this from hard toilsome experience. Another plan was to conceal ourselves in one of the side passages and trust to luck for the ducks coming within reach; or to make our way from channel to channel in hope of getting within gunshot. But so wary and cautious has long experience made the ducks, that neither of these schemes offer much hopes of success.

Not having any decoys with us, there remained nothing to be done but to plant an ambush and endeavor to drive the ducks into it. This was the plan we decided on—and now to carry it out. With the aid of a field-glass we could distinctly see our expected prey sunning themselves on a low bank on the south side of the farther end of the lagoon. It was evident, then, that our ambush must be placed up this way, while the rest of the party endeavored to get beyond the ducks and drive them along. At this end the pond narrowed to an opening not more than half a gunshot across. Here would be a splendid place to plant our ambush; and if we can only succeed in driving the ducks this far, the day is ours.

It was worth trying, at any rate; so we deposit Xavier on one side of the strait, the Professor on the other, while the rest of us make our way down the lagoon. At a respectful distance from the enemy we turn down a creek into the rushes and endeavor to force our way along the narrow, intricate passages until we can outflank them.

Then came the tug of war. The Captain was leading in the canoe, while Zeno and I did our best to follow with the lumbering punt. It was heavy work. Sometimes in a place where the canoe would pass with ease the boat would stick fast; the Captain would have to come to the rescue, and it required a great deal of pulling, hauling, and poling, to force the old thing along. At the same time we had to work in perfect silence, lest a vigilant foe should discover our plot and take the alarm. And it favored us immensely when a slight breeze sprang up and rustled the leaves in a manner which effectually drowned any noise we might make. At every passage we passed leading to the main channel, the Captain would proceed cautiously to reconnoitre and report our progress. At last we reached a bay where the lagoon seemed suddenly to terminate, and after a careful scrutiny the Captain informed us that we had passed the ducks by at least a hundred yards. This was good news; everything was blooming; now we prepared for the attack. A quantity of reeds and rushes were gathered and spread over the boat so that the hull was entirely covered, and green bushes were arranged so as to effectually conceal the fighting crew. Just here another question demanded consideration. Suppose, when this disguised affair should come sweeping along, the ducks, not liking the appearance of things, instead of passing up the pond, should endeavor to escape down one of those side channels, would not all our plotting and scheming be in vain?

Our ready Captain had foreseen the difficulty and

prepared for it. Zeno and I were to take the boat and keep the ducks as near as possible the south shore; while he would take the canoe and meet them at every channel if they should attempt to escape that way. Everything seemed favorable to the success of our enterprise; even the wind was in our favor, and would carry us gently along, leaving us nothing to do but to steer the concern.

When all was ready, forth we sallied. A vigorous push from the Captain sent us well out into the pond, where we caught the breeze and began to move slowly toward the unsuspecting water-fowl. It is doubtful if such a nondescript appearance as we presented was ever before seen in those waters. Zeno lay in the bow, completely covered with rushes, with the muzzle of his gun pointing ahead like a bowsprit; I had to admonish him to draw it in, lest the ducks should recognize it and make off too quickly. I sat in the stern, steering the boat, so embowered with spruce bows that I was scarcely sure of my own identity. Now all eyes to the front to watch the success of our ruse.

There on a low, flat bank scarcely rising above the water, is a large flock of ducks, and we are moving slowly but surely toward them. So complete is our disguise that for some time they pay no attention to us, and we begin to fear that our scheme will only prove too successful. At length as our suspicious-looking craft draws near, there is a decided commotion among them; toilet is abandoned; mud grubbing is laid aside; while all energies are bent to the scrutiny of the approaching *un*natural phenomenon. In the foreground, nearest to the water's edge, there posts a handsome bird of the masculine persuasion, which seems to be officiating as outside guard; for it is his warning voice that gives the first intimation of something unusual on foot. Judging from his appearance and bearing, he must be a bird of importance, probably the Nestor of the flock; a venerable drake whose opinion carries weight in the aquatic community. The uncommon occurrence of such a thing as an island breaking loose from its moorings, and starting off on a career of its own, appears to him decidedly irregular and highly reprehensible. So he loudly quacks his disapproval, emphasizing his remarks with some energetic bobbings of his wise old head, and some expressive waggles of his curly tail. The conclusion he came to was, that floating islands had better be avoided until you know more about them. So he took to the water, followed by the entire flock; and away they went, huddling close together, and looking back over their shoulders in a manner expressive of the greatest curiosity and amazement. They were not alarmed, but only suspicious, which was quite sufficient for our purpose if it only lasted long enough.

Now that we had them fairly before the wind, there was nothing to do but to steer as quietly as possible, and glide noiselessly along until we drew them within reach of our concealed comrades, and then, with concentrated fire, to retrieve the disasters of the past and furnish our pantry with duck enough for a week. So with almost imperceptible motion the mysterious island crept along. As we passed one of the side channels they made a movement as though about to seek shelter in that direction, but evidently discovered something down there more alarming than a floating heap of bulrushes, for they came out more quickly than they went in; this assured us that our vigilant Captain was on the *qui vive* and keeping well abreast; so that our final success seemed now certain.

How friend Zeno managed to keep quiet all this time with a score of fat ducks under the muzzle of his gun, is a most surprising thing; the self-control which he manifested on that trying occasion bodes well for his final reformation.

He ventured once to relieve his feelings by drawing back the rushes and revealing a visage which was positively crimson in the effort he was making to subdue his emotions. Not daring to utter a word, he favored me with a wink and a grimace that spoke volumes.

Now an explanation is required concerning the state of affairs at the other end of the lake. We have mentioned the narrow outlet where we had posted our reserve; it is to be hoped their patience is not yet exhausted; but by this time they have us well in sight and can amuse themselves by watching the progress of events. At this end the lagoon suddenly narrowed, after the fashion of the Mediterranean where it connects with the Atlantic. On the north side of the outlet was a bold rock, bearing some resemblance to Gibraltar.

Here we had posted the Professor, armed with a double-barrelled, long-range duck shooter; and we had an occasional glimpse of his head as he peered over his breastwork to watch our advance.   On the other side the Pillar of Hercules, so to speak, there crouched the active Xavier.   Now, to carry out the analogy, there was a flat rocky island, considerably to the east of them, which we decided to name Malta.   Here is where we met with the first hitch in our arrangements.   As we came sweeping along the Mediterranean, with the hostile squadron in full retreat, they put into Malta for shelter, and manifested a decided intention of proceeding no farther without first knowing the reason.   As we drew near, they very prudently withdrew to the far side of the rock; and, thinking they might dodge us round the island and get away, I brought the craft to a halt and held a whispered consultation with my second in command.   As might be expected, he was for advancing at all hazards.   But as that would have the effect of scattering the ducks, and perhaps losing them, I hesitated.   While we were lying there thinking over the matter, we noticed that the Gibraltar detachment was in motion, evidently contemplating an attack by land.   The Professor had left his post and was crawling along the rocks to get within range. He reaches the point on the mainland nearest to the island, and there he plants his battery and opens fire, so to speak.   It is a pretty long shot; but if any one can do it, it is the Professor.   He works that gun to the utmost it is capable of, and the result is that several ducks are kicking on their backs, while the rest take to flight in a westerly direction. "Have we lost them?"

Not yet: Xavier springs to his feet; and long before they are within range the excited Frenchman blazes away and yells. It has the desired effect, however, for their course is suddenly changed to the south-east; and there among the rushes our Captain, in his canoe, lurks like a Barbary pirate on the watch for unwary mariners. A double shot scatters death among them and once more changes their course. Now in their panic they seem to have forgotten all about the mysterious foe, and are coming straight toward us. "Be propitious, oh ye fates! they will be right over our heads." "Here they are: 'up, guards, and at them!'" We spring to our feet. A rattling bang! bang! closes the fusilade, and for a moment it seemed to be raining ducks. One fat old fellow came down so direct that he hit friend Zeno plump in the middle of his blooming countenance. That was all we were able to do. We had brought down eleven altogether; and, as the survivors in their retreat crossed a cliff several hundred feet in height, we decided to abandon the pursuit for the present.

N. B.—Our losses were slight.

It was an impressive sight just after the battle to witness the reunion of the scattered forces.

Great historical events of this kind are generally immortalized by the divine art of the painter; as in the instance of the meeting of Wellington and Blucher after Waterloo. As no poet or painter will ever immortalize this great event, it rests for my feeble pen to describe the grand gathering of the victorious legions. And it was a scene to be remembered when the Captain paddled out of the bulrushes, taking on board the North African garrison, and joined the mustering forces at the base of Gibraltar.

Zeno and I got there as quickly as we could with our floating masquerade. Then, with our eleven ducks laid in a row before us, we sat down on the rocks and renewed the sinews of war with the contents of our pockets. That closed our duck-hunting for the day. Before dismissing the subject, we might observe that a little while after we discovered a lake several miles away, abounding with water fowl which were not nearly so shy. And at any time, by sending a detachment of two for a day, we could generally supply ourselves with duck enough to keep up the variety.

CHAPTER VII.

NIMROD SEES A SPOOK.

ONE striking feature of these northern forests is the extreme solitude that everywhere prevails, the death-like stillness that broods over lake and mountain. In a tropical forest, we are told, day and night the air is filled with the clatter and din of animal life. How different here, where silence seems enthroned. Broken for a while by the report of one of our guns, there is a rumbling among the peaks and crags far and near, which gradually dies away, and silence which might be felt once more resumes its sway, until it is again disturbed in a similar manner. As we crossed and recrossed the extensive lake, and wound among the islands; or as we rambled over the mainland to distant lakes, and made long excursions among the woods and mountains, we discovered no trace of human beings besides ourselves. Ascending to the summits of lofty hills, we would survey vast expanses of wild landscape stretching on every hand to the far distant horizon; at one sweep

the eye would take in stretches of dark pine woods,
broken by towering crags, and intersected by rivers and
lakes, but nowhere resting upon a single mark that
betokened the presence of beings like ourselves. The
country was, to all appearance, as bare of humanity as
though man had never been created. It was to us as
though the great seething, toiling masses of a sin-cursed
race had passed away forever, and we alone were left .
in a world of solitude. It was a novel experience, to
say the least of it, and gave rise to thoughts and emotions to the contemplative mind that are seldom
experienced in the ordinary walks of life. Some might
be disposed to consider it a privilege to step aside out
of the rush of life, and have time and opportunity to
think and meditate without the least danger of disturbance; and the reader will, perhaps, be surprised to
hear that we have never found quiet seclusion to be
any help to study and meditation, but quite the reverse.
" As iron sharpeneth iron, so doth the countenance of
a man his friend;" and we have always found the
busy rush of earth's duties, the harsh jarring of the
wheels of time, the din and commotion of the crowded
city, to be far more stimulating to mental activity than
the drowsy solitude of rural retirement. Your rustic
philosopher is apt to be somewhat soporific.

As day after day and night after night wore away
in this region of loneliness, our connection with the
great busy world seemed to grow fainter and fainter,
until its memory only lingered as a troubled dream.
There were occasions when the solitude was certainly

oppressive, to the most ardent lover of nature, and we discovered that the contemplation of nature's marvels was, in the long run, a poor substitute for all the pleasures of social life.

The feeling of loneliness was most oppressive at night, if one should happen to awake after the camp was at rest. Whenever this happened to myself it was quite a disaster, for I could seldom get to sleep again for a long time; the thoughts and feelings I have had during those trying occasions would fill quite a volume if they had been caught at the time. For hours together I have lain listening to the regular breathing of my slumbering comrades, and watching their prostrate forms in the hope that one of them would awake and bear me company. Wearied of this, I would slip back the door of the tent and look out on the moonlit surface of the lake, finding the burden of solitude increasing as I traced out the windings among the islands lit up by the silvery moonbeams. What glorious nights those were; the full-orbed and radiant moon sweeping through a cloudless sky, holding her silent watch over a silent world; so perfectly was her rounded form reflected in the depths of the silent lake that there seemed to be another moon threading her way among the islands. Was there ever such brilliant moonlight?

"'Twas but the daylight sick."

Over the wild landscape was this flood of glory poured until the outlines of the cliffs were as plainly discernible as in broad day, and around the shadows of the islands was thrown a halo of silvery light. A picture to inspire the poet and the painter. But, oh! the solitude. It was not in the least relieved by the silent fluttering of a bat, so near to the door that I distinctly felt the wind of its wings and just got a view of its hideous form. "Thou imp of darkness, fit shape to symbolize the presiding genius of this lonely place!"

A gentle breeze to stir the needles of the pine, to ripple the surface of the lake, or rustle the walls of the tent would have been a relief; even the hooting of the owl would have been a welcome sound as indicating the presence of some kind of life. But it was most oppressive to find oneself the only living and moving being in a world of silence.

Enough of this. Let me follow the examples of my comrades and seek the land of nod; perhaps in my dreams I shall meet with congenial souls who will help to lighten the burden of my loneliness. So I roll my blanket around me and take to the twigs to make one more effort to redeem the night. But all in vain. No more sleep for me; so let me compose myself to the situation. I will fold back the door of the tent and let in some moonlight; perhaps I shall not feel so lonely if I can see something besides the distorted images of my own disordered imagination. There, now, I can see you all, if that is any comfort. Captain, Zeno, Professor, are all lying in the order named; and across at the other side lies Xavier, who slept in the tent for two wet nights, and has continued the privilege ever since.

Now let me give up sleep and have a think. Of all our wide realm of literature I can only think of one work that is at all apropos to the present situation, and that is a dreamy little work entitled "Zimmerman on Solitude," written, no doubt, in a back attic of some crowded city. If the drowsy old gentleman had experienced a few nights like this it would have given an additional emphasis to his rhapsodies. For our part, we are disposed to consider the whole thing a delusion and a snare. Our sentiments are more in harmony with those of that other individual who exclaimed so feelingly:

> "Oh! solitude, where are the charms
> That sages have seen in thy face?"

There is something almost weird about this silence; it is too intense to be natural. From the mere want of material to work up, the mind naturally produces its own, and peoples this fantastic region with fancies and figures of its own creation.

> "Look out through the radiance, so bold and so bright;
> Shine not, thou sweet moon, with so solemn a light.
> How lonesome! how wild!
> Yet the stillness is rife
> With the stir of the living—
> The spirit of life."

It was even so; the silence was positively suspicious. There is a striking incident recorded in one of Mr. Cooper's novels. A young scout had been sent to scrutinize what was supposed to be the lurking place of a party of hostile Indians. On his return he reported that all was quiet; but added that it was too quiet, he did not like such silence, it wasn't natural.

So it was on this occasion. Out of the intense silence there grew upon me the consciousness of a strange presence. What first occasioned it I knew not; but it gradually dawned upon me that some one or something was near. Spirit or mortal I knew not, but only that there was a mysterious presence. I must have been at that moment in the state of mind into which the dupes of spiritualism are brought, when they are expected to accept those wonderful manifestations from the spirit world; for I would have received almost any thing that could have been presented just then, as a relief from the insufferable solitude: so that, as I slowly opened my eyes, I was not much surprised or startled to see, strongly defined in the patch of moonlight on the opposite wall of the tent, the profile of a human face.

But whose? In a flash my mind took in all the difficulties that were against a bodily presence in that place. The unscalable cliff, the lake without a boat, the impassable ravine at the back; there was no possible way by which a human being could have invaded us in this manner. But there was the shadow, plainer than the nose on the faces of some men. My next thought was: "I am dreaming." No, I am lying on my back with my hands beneath my head; I can distinctly feel a twig sticking into my ribs. I am wide awake, staring with all my might at that inscrutable shadow thrown by the moonlight on the wall of the— No, it is not there! Where did it go? It certainly was there, only for a moment, but in that moment I thought all that is written here and a great deal more. And now it is gone as quickly and as noiselessly as it came. I can feel the perspiration trickling from every part of my body, which is enough to convince me that something unusual has happened; so I reach over and shake my nearest bedfellow, whispering:

"Captain, there's a man in the camp."

"The d——!" said the Captain, starting to a sitting posture.

"No," said I, "I don't think it was him. Though I did not recognize the party."

"You must be dreaming, boy. There is not a man within twenty miles of us, and if there were he could not get here without wings."

"I have thought of all that, Captain, and still I positively declare that a man looked into the tent and left the shadow of his ugly phiz on that patch of moonlight."

The Captain here turned round and gave his neighbor a thump on the back, exclaiming:

"Zeno, wake up, old man; here's a pretty mess we are in. Nimrod says there's a man in the camp."

Zeno gave a lazy roll over, and slowly rose to his hands and knees, repeating in a dazed manner: "A man in the camp?"

When the seriousness of the situation had fairly dawned upon him, he sprang to his feet, exclaiming:

7

"By the great Jumbo! what does he want? Look out for the guns, Captain."

So saying he rushed out of the tent. We all followed, including the Professor and Xavier, who had been aroused.

We made our way first to the recess under the cliff where our guns and ammunition had been stored; but nothing was disturbed in that quarter. A careful examination of the surroundings of the camp gave us no light on the dark mystery. We searched the grass and sand for the trace of a strange foot-print; and even lighted a couple of torches and examined the thick carpet of needles for some distance into the grove. The utmost that rewarded our search was a faint indication of the needles being disturbed by a trail leading in a direction in which we seldom went; but whether of man or beast we could not determine. Returning to the camp, Xavier met us with the information that his department had been invaded; which was proved by the fact that a partridge and a black bass, which had been suspended from the limb of a birch, had been carried off. After surveying the scene of the depredation, the Captain gave his opinion that a wild cat or a wolverine could easily have done that. This appeared probable from the fact that a knife and hatchet which were sticking in the bark of the same tree had not been disturbed. But on this supposition, the greatest mystery of all, the shadow in the tent, remained unaccounted for. I was eager to seize on everything which went to indicate that I had not

been deceived, as some of my comrades seemed to con-
clude, and proposed that we have another look at that
trail, and get the opinion of Xavier, who was the most
experienced bushman among us. The wily Frenchman went down on his knees and scrutinized the
mark with the intense, fixed gaze of a bank teller
examining a doubtful signature. Zeno sarcastically
recommended that we bring out the microscope to aid
the study. To which the Professor added, that we
had better take home a specimen of that track and
subject it to a chemical analysis. But there was very
little that we could learn; the soft springy needles did
not retain a foot-print that could be recognized. There
was only an indication that they had been disturbed
by something passing over them, but whether man or
beast we could not determine. Indeed, the super-
stitious Frenchman ventured the opinion that it was
neither.

There was nothing for us to do but to give up the
search till daylight, and then institute a minute investi-
gation until the dark mystery was unravelled.

As we came back to the camp there were a number
of witty allusions made to my sharp sight or strong
imagination, though they paid enough deference to my
testimony to bring their guns into the tent and spend
the rest of the night on the look-out. Fortunately, by
this time it was near morning; the moon had already
descended beyond the western horizon, and the eastern
sky was tinged with a roseate hue, betokening the
approaching dawn. So we sat in the tent and told
wonderful stories of forest mysteries until the glorious

up-soaring of the king of day put the shadows to flight, and light, glorious light,

"Offspring of Heaven, first-born,"

was enthroned on the mountain's crest. What a different world it seemed in broad daylight! How easy it was to laugh at the terrors of the night, now the darkness had flown away and the woods and islands were basking in the glowing sunbeams. The first thing to be attended to, of course, was breakfast; nothing short of a convulsion of nature would move us to abandon that order of things. So breakfast came on as though nothing unusual was stirring in our little world; and the respect we paid to it indicated that the excitement of the previous night had not in any way impaired our appetites.

Breakfast over, we commenced our reconnaissance to discover, if we could, what mysterious foe had invaded the privacy of our solitude. Many were the regrets expressed that we had not the service of our sharp-scented dog, whose natural instinct would have been of great assistance to us in ferreting out the intruder. But that sagacious creature was absent with Narcisse and Old Nick, on their unknown business; so we have to do the best we can with our own natural faculties. Inch by inch, and yard by yard, we explored the ground in widening circles around our tent. But the only trace we could discover of our invisible friend or foe was the trail through the pines, which we had examined in the darkness; and upon this trail we now concentrated all our attention. So poorly paid were we for all our trouble that we were on the point of giving up the search in despair, trusting to the intruder making his appearance again the following night. I had been leaning against a tree, studying the matter with all the mental power I was capable of, when an idea struck me which seemed to lighten the mystery somewhat, and I stepped forward, exclaiming:

"See here, Professor; that trail was made by a man; I would stake my reputation on that."

"That is the very question at issue," replied the Professor.

"Well, I have come to that conclusion, and now I will give you my points." So saying, I placed myself beside the trail and walked cautiously forward, taking strides of the same length, which were rather long for me. The result was that I left a trail exactly like the one we were examining.

"That is point number one; now for the next. Do you see that fallen tree yonder? There is a space of three feet beneath it. A lynx or wolverine could pass beneath it quite easily; not so a man; he would very likely make a detour to avoid it, as you see is the case with this trail; point number two. See here, again. In stepping over this log he left the print of his foot close up on either side; a four-footed beast would have cleared it at a bound or leaped to the top and down again; point number three. And further, when he passed between two small trees he disturbed the twigs to the height of at least five feet."

"Bravo!" shouted Zeno; "encore! encore! Lead on, my noble Nimrod, we'll have him yet."

"There is not much more at present," I continued, "except that he was a tall man, and on this trail he was approaching our camp, but did not come back this way."

"How do you make that out?"

"Easily enough," I explained. "These strides were not taken by a small man; and only a long-legged individual could have stepped over that log without making a mark on the moss. As to direction, you will observe that in these needles we sink an inch deep at every step, and as the foot is lifted the needles about the toe are turned over, thus indicating the direction in which we are proceeding."

Friend Zeno had taken in all these points with intense interest, and the last observation appeared to cause him immense delight.

"I declare," he shouted, "if it is not as good as a book. Nimrod, my boy, you have mistaken your calling. You should have been a detective or an Indian hunter. But go on, old fellow. What's the shade of his hair and the color of his eyes?"

"You should have asked that question last night when he inserted his ugly mug into our tent."

Our worthy Captain here came forward to have a word in the discussion.

"If I may venture an opinion," said he, "his hair and his eyes are both black."

"Why so, Captain?"

"Because he must be either an Indian or the devil; and there is a strong family resemblance between them."

From this observation it will be inferred that our genial Captain, with all his good-nature, had no great love for the aboriginal denizens of the forest. This peculiarity he had in common with most lumbermen, and when their reasons are given it is not surprising that such is the case.

The noble red man of Fennimore Cooper is a creature of the imagination. If he ever did exist in flesh and blood, he is now no more. The Indian of to-day, in his wild state, is a wretched sneak-thief; a disgusting, cowardly, mischief-making rascal, who sneaks around lumber camps and settlements, stealing everything he can carry off; hooking sheep, pigs, and chickens, and making himself a general nuisance. He comes to the shanty in midwinter in a destitute condition, pretending to be doubled up with starvation. He wheedles the good-natured cook out of a feed and a warm, and sits by the caboose eating baked beans and pork with a bearing as meek and demure as a charity girl. An unsophisticated observer would imagine that evil was far from his guileless heart. But all the while he is making an inventory of all the movable articles within reach; and when he has stowed away enough pork and beans for a week, should the cook's back be turned for a moment, the disgraceful scallawag is off to the bush with a hop, step, and a jump, bearing with him some useful souvenir of his visit.

No wonder there is little love for the poor Indian in the lumberman's heart. I have heard them uttering their opinion of the noble savage in language more expressive than elegant; and sometimes even regretting that they were not free to clear off the pesky vermin along with the skunks and raccoons.

A member of this interesting family had stolen a march on us.

"But where did he come from?" inquired the Professor.

"That's not the question," replied the Captain. "Where did he go to is the mystery. He came down here to our camp, helped himself to our provisions, and we can discover no trace of his return. He must either have vanished into the air or waltzed off on the water. Anyhow, we are not safe here any more. They will steal all we have and starve us to death. We shall have to keep a sharp look-out every night, and if he comes again fill him up with buckshot."

In this pleasant condition the interesting subject will have to be left at present.

CHAPTER VIII.

"*LO! THE POOR INDIAN.*"

SEVERAL nights passed after the events narrated in our last without any further disturbance. We each took our turn at watching the camp during the hours of darkness, but nothing came of it beyond a great deal of vexation and loss of sleep. One morning, a little before noon, I was fishing along the base of the cliff just where the rocky path suddenly terminated, a place where I have frequently had good success. There I was fishing away, paying all attention to the work in hand, when a shadow fell on the water beside me. Just then I had a bite, and, thinking the shadow was caused by some one from the camp, I did not look round immediately, but kept my gaze fixed on the line till my quarry was fairly hooked; then, lifting it out of the water, I turned to the unknown at my side with a smile of triumph, when —astonishment, surprise, amazement! neither of these words, nor all of them, will express the state of my mind at finding myself confronted with the most startling apparition that ever fell upon these eyes. I stood for a moment petrified, with my fish dangling in the air. Such a wild, brigandish-looking mortal was never seen outside a menagerie.

.It was an Indian, to be sure; probably the very one we have been hunting for so long turning up when least expected.

How shall I begin to describe the nondescript figure he presented. The costume comes first, of course. To describe it in a word, I would say that it consisted mainly of holes fastened together with thongs of raw hide. "Nature abhors a vacuum," said the old philosophers. But this degenerate child of nature displayed a sublime disregard of vacuums of every shape and dimension. Perhaps a little more of detail is required; so let me begin at the top and work down. His head was covered with a thick mat of tangled black hair, which looked as though it had been combed with a garden rake and brushed out with the broom; it grew to an equal length all over his head, and was distributed as it grew without any reference to fore and aft, so that his twinkling black eyes peeped out through the ragged thatch—

"Like to an owl in ivy bush."

The upper part of his body was covered with an old blue woollen jersey, the numerous holes in which revealed the fact that it was the sole garment in that vicinity. His legs and feet were protected by leggings and mocassins of untanned moose hide, in very reduced circumstances. The rather large interval between the bottom of his jersey and the top of his leggings was provided for in a manner in which the maximum of ingenuity combined with the minimum of material; and the whole of his costume displayed a disregard for such trifles as fresh air and daylight that was suggestive of a lofty mind. By way of ornaments, this "Old man of the Mountain" sported a necklace of birds' beaks, bears' claws, human teeth, and other jewels; across his breast, as became a nobleman of nature, he wore a rare display of medals and decorations, composed mainly of the lids of tin blacking-boxes. Over his right shoulder was thrown with courtly grace a ragged blanket, while his left arm flourished an old flint-lock musket. This weapon, from its venerable appearance, might have scattered death at the battle of Quebec. If so, its ferocious air and immense proportions readily explain the sudden rout of the French. No reasonable man could expect them to stand before such formidable-looking weapons. An empty powder-horn and a sheath knife completed the *tout ensemble* of my new acquaintance. As to personal appearance, he was fully six feet tall, with a gaunt, long frame, flat, repulsive features, and a complexion which indicated that one great struggle of his life had been to keep out of the water.

This was the spectre that had thrust itself upon my attention; a dirty, greasy, half-naked savage, whose filthy person seemed to defile the very sunlight that fell upon him.

However, we are constitutionally so courteous and affable that it is not in our nature to be uncivil to any-

thing, even to such a dirty dog as this; so we lower
our unlucky fish that has been dangling in the air all
this time, take off our chapeau with all the grace we
are capable of, and make our obeisance to this scion of
the woods, stating at the same time that we were
proud to make his acquaintance. His reply was
given in a language I could not understand; but I
presume he was saying that the feeling was reciprocal.
After exchanging a few expressions of mutual respect
and esteem, we stood gazing at each other. I was
mentally wondering what was next demanded by the
etiquette of the forest. Just then on the balmy air
was borne the welcome call to dinner. I informed my
guest what that sound meant, and, stating that I could
not think of dining without my worthy friend, begged
that he would allow me to escort him to the dining-
room. After walking a few paces with that spectre
at my heels, it occurred to me that I would be more
comfortable if that murderous-looking musket were in
advance, so I paused and motioned him to lead the
way, which he readily did. They were all on the
grass before the tent, each with his plate between his
knees; but the expression on their countenances as I
advanced to present our guest would have made a
study for Hogarth.

"Gentlemen," said I, bowing with mock gravity,
"allow me to present to you the celebrated Mr. Lo,
the famous individual renowned in prose and poetry
as nature's nobleman."

This would perhaps have caused a laugh had not

their surprise been too great for any other feeling. The Captain was the first to recover his power of speech.

"Nimrod, you son of a gun, where in the world did you find that scarecrow?"

"Hush! Captain, don't hurt the gentleman's feelings; you ought to be proud to make his acquaintance, he is a real aristocrat, a knight of the Order of Boot Blacking, as you see by his regalia."

Xavier was coming from the kitchen with a plate in each hand, when he encountered this unsavory phantom; the shock was so great that he stopped abruptly, deposited the plates on the grass, and drew back with a look of the most intense astonishment on his visage. This our noble visitor interpreted as an invitation to fall to. So he threw aside his gun and blanket with great alacrity, dropped on his knees, and, seizing both plates, he emptied one into the other and fell to, *sans ceremonie.*

Those plates with their contents were originally intended for Zeno and me; and it looked as though our chances for dinner were slight indeed. Zeno broke out at last,—

"Well, may I be smothered in honey if that doesn't beat any pantomime I ever heard of! I say, Nimrod, that must be one of your distinguished relations; no wonder you are so awfully stiff."

Fortunately the infallible Xavier had a supply in reserve, so Zeno and I were provided with something to begin on; and when dinner was in progress I told them all I knew about that itinerant nightmare.   Before the rest of us had fairly commenced he had finished his double portion ; and after carefully licking out the plate he laid it on the grass and looked about him with an Oliver Twist expression of countenance.

"Get him some more, Xavier," cried Zeno, with a chuckle. "Sixpence extra to see the animal feeding. Captain, I'd give a dollar to see how much he would stick into that carcase."

Our indignant cook came out of the kitchen with a collection of fragments, which he pitched down on the grass as though he were feeding a dog, grumbling all the time, in most expressive French, at having to wait on such disreputable company.   It was not long until the very last of these was demolished, and still our insatiate guest appeared as lean and hungry as though he had eaten nothing for a week.

"Encore, Xavier !" shouted Zeno.   "Captain, let us see this thing out."

"Hold," said the Captain ; "that will do. I tell you, Zeno, you don't know these people.   That fellow would eat all we have in the camp if we gave it him ; he would eat till his pantaloons would not hold him. That is their style ; when they have anything to eat, they eat it all, and then starve till they get some more. A fellow of that kind once crawled through the window of my provision store, and ate till he was too big to get out again ; and there we found him in the morning, so full that he could hardly move. Now, let me have a talk to that chap. I want to find out some-

thing about him." So saying he addressed himself to
the worthy child of the forest.

After considerable palaver, he discovered that the
stranger had a little knowledge of French and expressed himself open to negotiation. He accounted
for his presence there by the statement that he fell
over the cliff, and had been concealed behind a boulder
for three weeks without any food. He knew nothing
about the provisions we had lost, had never been near
our camp before to-day, and had had nothing to eat
for a month. He was quite alone, had got separated
from his tribe in the spring when they were out hunting, and had had nothing to eat ever since. He was a
big Indian, the chief of his tribe, and his name was
Tzoobloowootskibuchram. He was the bravest warrior
in all the world. He was the greatest hunter that
ever lived. He had slaughtered deer by thousands,
and had slain more bears than the leaves of the forest.
But now that his powder-horn was empty, and the
silent mountains no longer echoed the death-shot of
the mighty chief, the deer laughed at him, the bear
mocked him ; even the night owl said " too-whoo " in
derision, because he was weak and starved, and had
had nothing to eat for six months. This was the substance of all that could be extracted from him by the
most rigid examination, and the Captain was of the
opinion that it was not very reliable.

Still the brave warrior had eaten our salt, and we
were bound to treat him with becoming courtesy while
he remained with us ; the difficulty was, how to get rid

of him without hurting his aristocratic feelings. The
Captain proposed, at last, to send him to the opposite
side of the lake in the canoe, and letting him go about
his business ; and we, forthwith, prepared to give him
a send-off worthy of his rank and station. We replen-
ished his empty powder-horn, whereat the soul of the
mighty hunter sang for joy. We gave him a good
blanket in the place of the tattered rag he bore. We
put up several pounds of pork and biscuit to help him
on his journey home. And lastly, as a mark of our
esteem, we invested him with the Order of the Star of
Pickled Salmon, the insignia of which consisted of
tin can lids threaded on a string. This over, we
escorted him to the beach, where he took his seat in
the canoe in which Zeno and I were to row him away,
as we fondly, but vainly, hoped, never to return.

While crossing the lake we held quite a dialogue
with our illustrious passenger, from which we will give
a few brief extracts :

"Does not the soul of my red brother pine for the
smoke of his wigwam and the faces of his young
men ?"

" Ne pit skunk," was the musical reply ; which we
accepted as equivalent to " You bet, old hoss."

" And will not the heart of my brave old cocka-
lorum sometimes turn to his white brothers of the
canvas wigwam ?"

" Nickety pickawa cum sickerty kicka bung," or
something to that effect, shouted the doughty chief,
as he brandished aloft his old musket with his left
hand, while with his right he gave me a hearty grasp.

"Indeed, you quite surprise me. I scarcely expected such a demonstration of affection."

If that is what he meant it for, the dear fellow was as good as his word, and soon gave substantial proof that he loved us too dearly to stay away. As we landed him at the farthest part of the lake, I stepped ashore to bid him farewell, and thus addressed him :

"Free spirit of the mountains, depart in peace, bearing in thy gentle bosom the memory of the white man's kindness. Through the pathless woods and over the toilsome mountains make thy homeward way, pausing not till thy fleet foot has crossed the threshold of the distant wigwam in the village of thy fathers, where the weeping squaw, with tearful eyes, is watching in vain for her chief's return, and where the squalling papoose bewails the absence of its dad. Proud child of the desert, depart ; the star of peace direct thee ; and—good riddance to bad rubbish."

I delivered this exordium with uplifted hands and closed eyes, and was quite oblivious to the fact that the mighty skunk-hunter was off like a shot, without a parting word; so I had been wasting my sweetness on the desert air. I opened one eye near the end, and discovered his absence just in time to close in that rather abrupt manner.

"I say, Nimrod," called Zeno, "that's the most unceremonious chap I ever saw. He went up that slope like a singed cat ; and the ungrateful old scamp stopped and shook his knife at us in a most ferocious way. That's all we get by feeding and honoring such

8

cattle as that. Well for the old villain I hadn't a gun
or I would have given him a parting salute with a few
grains of lead."

We returned slowly to the camp and spent the rest
of the day in peace and quiet. We did not consider it
necessary to keep a watch that night, supposing we
had seen the last of the mysterious stranger.

The next day we were all away on the lake, the
camp being deserted for several hours. On our return
we were surprised and alarmed to see several persons
moving about. Two of them were exploring the
kitchen, apparently making free with the provisions;
several others were moving in and out of the tent.
This was an alarming state of things,. We concluded
at once they were Indians, and, putting all our strength
into oar and paddle, made all possible speed to the
landing. Before we could get near enough to recognize any of them a shout was raised by someone, evidently on the look-out, and the whole company trooped
off to the forest.

" The thieving rascals," growled the Captain, "they'll
steal all we have. Give way, boys."

As we struck the beach a dilapidated individual
emerged from the tent, whom we recognized as our
visitor of the preceding day. He gave us a whoop of
defiance, brandishing his murderous-looking musket
with a war-like air, and started off on the trail of his
retreating band. But he seemed to have been seized
with paralysis in his legs, for they shook and bent
beneath his weight. The grotesque appearance of

that long, gaunt figure, staggering and swaying up the slope, provoked a laugh from us all as we dashed. in pursuit.

Whatever it was that troubled the worthy chief he had it badly, for the very moment we laid our hands on him his legs seemed to shut up after the fashion of a carpenter's rule, and down he went on his hams with a thump. We had not expected such a sudden collapse. There he sat, swaying to and fro, with his hands energetically polishing the pit of his stomach as though he were disturbed by some internal sensations. We soon discovered that it was not anguish, but pleasure, he was experiencing. The grimaces that were distorting his rusty countenance were comical to witness, and of the torrent of gibberish that flowed incessantly from his lips the only syllable we could understand was a very expressive "hic," repeated at regular intervals, from all which signs we concluded that his lordship was not dying, but simply drunk.

No great mystery about that. We kept a bottle of brandy in the tent for cases of necessity. After six weeks in camp that bottle was still uncorked, and evidently fallen into the hands of the Philistines. The chief, of course, would come in for the lion's share, and the effect of the unaccustomed cordial was as described. It does not take much to make an Indian drunk; and when he is drunk he is the very drunkest of all possible drunks.

Finding that he was too helpless to move, we came back to the camp to ascertain our losses. Fortunately

our armory had not been discovered, so that our guns
and ammunition remained intact. The kitchen had
been pretty well cleaned out. But fortunately the
caution of Xavier had led him to store most of our
provisions in a secret recess under the cliff and keep in
the kitchen only the provision needed for each day's
consumption.

Now for the tent. They have evidently held high
carnival here. Our bags have all been opened and
their contents tumbled out on the floor. The Professor's field-glass they had evidently taken to be a kind
of double-barrelled brandy bottle, for they had taken
off the eye pieces, and the marks of their teeth showed
how they had been trying to pull out the corks. But
although very nearly everything had been overhauled,
very little, if anything, had been carried off. Either
the brandy bottles, bogus and genuine, had monopolized
their attention, or our unexpected return had discon-
certed their plans. Certainly we had reason to feel
thankful that we had suffered so little from this
unceremonious visit. "Now," said the Captain, when
we had reduced things to order, "we will hunt up
those fellows and ascertain how they came here."

"Captain, don't you think it possible they might
have come down from the rear; along the passage of
this water, for instance, there might be some kind of
ravine by which they could descend?" This inquiry
was made by the Professor, and it was an explanation
of the difficulty which had occurred to myself.

"No," was the reply; "we have explored up there;

nothing but an eagle could get down that way; the water tumbles over a rock fifty feet high; they must have a boat of some kind. Come along."

Xavier was left in charge of the camp with instructions to fire a shot if anything turned up while we were away. The doughty chief was lying just where he fell, calmly slumbering, so we left him there and pressed on in the trail of the others. We had no need of a great deal of skill to follow them, for there was as rough a track as though a brigade of cavalry had charged up the slope. Our common ideas about the airy foot and stealthy tread of the crafty red man may be very poetic and very romantic, but hardly true to nature; we have never seen an Indian yet who did not make a track that would shame a cow. As for their stealth and craft, the reader may judge of that when informed that we came suddenly upon the whole party when they were in the act of holding a council of war; the jabbering of their own voices drowned the noise of our approach, and our sudden appearance startled them as much as though we had dropped from the pine tops. They were nine in number, and a pretty scraggy-looking lot. With their attire modelled on the costume we have described in the early part of this chapter, as they squatted on the needles in a bunch, they certainly presented a wild and picturesque appearance. Only one man was furnished with a gun, and that looked as though it might be as safe at one end as at the other. There were several knives and hatchets among them, but on the whole a very poor display of weapons.

At our appearance they sprang to their feet and commenced to disperse; but a stern shout from the Captain, and a menacing movement of the barrel of his "long range," brought them to a standstill; another challenge, delivered in the Captain's deepest tones, induced them to commit an unconditional surrender.

I could not help thinking that the Indian's courage and spirit had been very much overrated when I saw our Captain, not by any means a large man, walk into the midst of those knives and hatchets and single out the biggest Indian of the pack for a parley. There were fiery gleams in some of their eyes, and some of their hands played rather threateningly about the handles of their sheath-knives; but that dark frown on the white man's face cowed the bravest spirit among them.

Then followed quite a lengthy palaver. It was surprising how much jabbering it took to elicit the smallest amount of information.

We learned at last that they belonged to a tribe situated near Lake Temiscaming, about a hundred and fifty miles to the north-west of us; and they were out on their summer ramble. These wretched creatures lived during the winter, partly supported by the Government, partly by trapping for the Hudson Bay Company, or hunting moose for the lumbermen, making up whatever else they needed by stealing anything they could. During summer, when game and fish were plentiful, they prowled about the woods in parties and lived pretty much as we saw them. As to how they

came there, we were informed that they came down
by the water. Nothing further could be learned from
them, and indeed nothing more was needed; so they
were ordered to take themselves off, and threatened
with every possible penalty short of instant annihila-
tion if they ever dared to come there again.

As the ragged squad withdrew, apparently well
pleased to get off so easily, we followed to ascertain how
they really did effect their entrance. In a few minutes
we came to the cliff, by the side of which ran the water
course. From the worn appearance of the rocks it
was evidently a considerable stream in some seasons,
but now only an almost imperceptible rill trickled from
stone to stone; and the empty channel formed a convenient stairway up the precipice. For about a
hundred yards our course lay by the side of the cliff,
and suddenly turning to the left we find an immense
chasm in the precipice down which the water seems to
have made its way. This rift in the mountain contains a reservoir of clear, still water several feet deep,
and we have a very narrow footing along its border.
Edging along sideways we make our way for several
yards, and at last there is no help for it but to take
to the water and wade across, leg deep, to the other
side, where we crawl on hands and knees under the
overhanging cliff, till we reach the farther end of the
chasm, and find all farther progress barred by a smooth,
slippery rock forty feet high. Now, how did they
get down into this place and how did they get up
again ? The mystery is easily solved, for a spruce has

tumbled into the ravine, the branches of which would assist an active climber in getting up and down.

However, a few blows with an axe will bring that tree into the water and make all secure in that direction. So we retrace our slippery steps and make our way home again, where we find Xavier keeping guard, while the prostrate Indian lie where we left him, snoring as hard as ever.

To dismiss the subject, before closing the chapter we have only to state that on awakening from his drunken stupor, we conveyed him once more across the lake and gave him his *mittimus*. The Captain and Xavier were for giving him a good thrashing before parting with him. But this was opposed by the Professor and myself, and in the end merciful measures prevailed. The Captain was fain to content himself with the energetic performance of a ceremony which is sometimes described as introducing the boot-maker to the tailor; at the same time bidding the fellow to "get to your own parish."

Sic transit Mr. Lo, and the brief acquaintance has not raised his character much in our estimation. There is certainly a great deal of gushing sympathy and maudlin admiration wasted over the noble red man, which he is not entitled to. If he has any virtues when he is converted and civilized, then give all the glory to that gospel which has saved him, for the fact remains that in his natural state the Indian is about as disreputable a scoundrel as ever decorated a gallows.

CHAPTER IX.

E had not been favored much with the society of Narcisse and Nicholas since coming into camp; they had been employed most of the time in opening a bush road to facilitate lumbering operations the following winter. Occasionally they would look in upon us to receive orders from the Captain, and lend whatever assistance we required; their appearance in camp was generally an event of interest, as they invariably came loaded with supplies from the castle, and with game they had taken.

After a while, however, we had reason to suspect that they were engaged in operations considerably more interesting than road-making. They made their appearance with greater frequency, and there was an air of secrecy about all their doings which excited our curiosity. We could not understand why the peaceful enterprize of clearing bush should require so much ammunition as they appeared to use, or why they should be favored with the services of the dog while the camp went unguarded day and night. All these things led us to suppose there was a little side play going on, and we naturally became very curious to learn what it was.

At last the revelation was made. The two supposed wood-choppers arrived in camp one afternoon with haste in their movements, mystery on their countenances, and an air of importance generally. They had a long private conference with the Captain, at the close of which they took the canoe and returned across the lake at a high rate of speed.

The Captain then called us all about him and favored us with an explanation of the business, the substance of which was as follows: It seems, that in the course of their rambles, these two wandering spirits had come across the track of some bears, and, thinking it might be agreeable to the Captain, had furnished him with information to that effect. The Captain immediately commissioned them to suspend operations, and put themselves upon the trail of those bears, to trace them out, to find their haunts, to study their habits, and make every arrangement for bringing us to where we could catch them with the least amount of trouble. This was the kind of work that had been going on for some time, and, in order to surprise us, the Captain had kept the affair secret until all his plans were completed. Now, it seemed, the time had come for striking the decisive blow.

The persevering Frenchmen had traced out the meandering trail of those bears day after day, and, having discovered their present locality, they had watched their operations until they knew pretty well every move the bears were likely to make, so there seemed every probability of their being able to bring us into contact with very little delay.

The bears were four in number, male and female, and two cubs. They were in the habit of resorting at sundown to a den among the mountains, the exact locality of which had been distinctly marked down. Now, the plan proposed was for us all to proceed well armed to the spot, in the night, and surround the mouth of the den before daylight, to shoot the two old bears as they emerged in the morning; and, if possible, to secure the two young ones alive.

I need not tell you we listened with considerable interest while the Captain unfolded these rather formidable plans. Now was the time he assured us; we would never have a better chance. If we had to hunt those bears for ourselves it would take us all summer, but it was a comparatively easy thing to bag the game when it was fairly run to earth. I need not tell you that there was not a dissentient voice: we were unanimous for war. We have not forgotten the rather peaceful sentiments that were uttered at the commencement of this history. The fact is, at starting, we had no anticipation of any such quarry as this, but now that it was thrown fairly into our hands, we were not slow to seize the rare opportunity.

Visions floated before our minds of bearskin rugs on the study floor, and formidable-looking claws and

teeth to exhibit to our admiring friends. Along with
this, there was the prospect of unlimited big talk
among the poor ordinary folks down below, who never
enjoyed the privilege of hunting the wild bear out of
his dark den.

All this was very nice indeed, but the bears were
not caught yet; and now and then the uncomfortable
thought occurred to us that they might not fall in
with our view of the case, and we are aware that bears
can raise a vigorous opposition against any measure
of which they do not approve.

Considerable weight is added to these reflections by
an examination of our armory. We are certainly not
fitted out for such heavy work, and for a moment we
doubt if we are justified in undertaking it. But war
is declared and hostilities have already commenced.
Narcisse is now on his way to the scene of action, to
watch the den and make sure they are within when
we arrive at early dawn; Nicholas has gone to the
castle to procure some articles needed for the expedition. That puts a new face on the matter, so we
proceed to survey our resources. There is a good
serviceable Snider in the shanty, which the Captain
generally uses on occasions of this kind. The Professor has a pet Remington, in the use of which he
claims to be expert, although he has done nothing with
it as yet beyond riddling pieces of birch bark at two
hundred yards; it seems a slight machine to attempt
the slaughter of a bear with, throwing a bullet not
much larger than a pea. That is really all the artil-

lery we can place in the field that can be depended on
for any long range. Beyond this we have nothing
but smooth-bores carrying home-made bullets. They
are pretty hard hitters for their kind, for the bullets
are full large, and they may do good execution at
short range; but short range with a pack of infuriated
bears is likely to be rather a trying situation for
amateur sportsmen. Fortunately there are plenty of
them; we have just enough artillery to go round, and
the Captain declares he will advance the entire company, including the dog, and the camp will have to
take care of itself.

Nicholas arrives from the castle with the Snider, a
bullet mould, and various other things; so we spend
the afternoon casting bullets and making all prepara-
tions for the work in hand.

The lair of the wild beasts is about ten miles from
here, and the route lies through such broken country
that, in order to get there before sunrise, we will have
to start about midnight. So as soon as the sun goes
down we turn in to have a few hours' sleep before
starting. Sleeping, under those circumstances, would
have been very difficult to most persons; but we had
become so accustomed to the vicissitudes of savage
life that we slept quite soundly till we were aroused
by a poke in the side, and found the Captain standing
over us, lighting his pipe, and at the same time stirring
up the company with the toe of his boot.

"Time to start, boys, and no time to lose."

It was rather trying to the patience to be roughly

shaken out of a sound slumber and called to leave the
warm blankets and go out into the chilly night air
for a long journey in the dark; but the thought of
our enterprise filled us with unusual vigor, and we
sprang up ready for action. We had made all pre-
parations over night, so there was no delay. Two
days' rations for the whole party were put up and
carried by Nicholas. Our stock of pine knots being
low, we reinforced them with rolls of birch bark and
turpentine. We needed plenty of light, for the moon
was down and the woods were filled with Egyptian
darkness.

Now, when all is ready, we take our seats in the
boat and are rowed gently across the lake, the muffled
rumbling of the oars being the only sound that broke
the stillness, and the only lights visible being the two
twinkling spots before the faces of the Captain and
Xavier. There seemed to be an unusual tendency to
speak in hushed murmurs and to remain as motionless
as possible, so that we would have presented a very
mysterious appearance to an observer had there been
any near.

Crossing the broad lagoon we had light enough
from the stars; but when we entered the channels
among the islands, where the cliffs sometimes leaned
over our heads and the branches of the trees frequently
brushed our faces, a light was needed to keep us from
running aground at every turn. The office of torch-
bearer was assigned to me, and as I sat in the bow
flourishing a flaming roll of birch, I enjoyed very

much the fantastic play of light and shadow on the rocks and trees we passed. We have no time for a detailed description; indeed, there was no time for a detailed observation, for all our faculties were required for the purposes of navigation. Travelling by water was a comparatively easy mode of procedure, and could we have covered the whole distance in that manner our labors would have been comparatively light. But when we landed from the boat and endeavored to push our way on foot through the gloomy forest then came the tug of war. We took the precaution to see that no gun was loaded, so as to avoid the danger of a premature discharge, lighted several torches and proceeded single file, Nicholas leading. For several miles we had a pleasant path through an open pine wood, and, with our glare of light and glittering arms, made quite an imposing array.

By this time our spirits were high and our hearts were light, and very soon we were beguiling the way by roaring songs in both French and English. Nicholas and Xavier were highly delighted when we made the pine woods ring with our college versions of "Allouette," " Vive la Canadienne," " Bon soir, mes amis, bon soir," and other roaring French choruses. And so, for an hour or more, the roaring, blazing brigade swept on, startling the quiet old forest with sights and sounds that had not been seen nor heard there since the creation.

But it was not going to be all so smooth sailing as this. In a little while we descended into a valley and

found ourselves in a beaver meadow. When we were
travelling waist-high through tangled grass wet with
dew, and where an occasional mis-step took one leg
deep in water, our merry ditties gave place to exclama-
tions of an entirely different character. Zeno and
I were travelling together in the line of march, and
the variety of expletives and interjections to which
that impatient youth gave utterance in the course of
an hour was a revelation of the resources of our grand
old Saxon tongue.

We need not drag the reader all through this weary
pilgrimage ; it will suffice to say that we were so free
with our torches that they gave out and left us in the
dark. We were having considerable trouble to get
along, and were despairing of arriving in time, when
we observed a light in the distance which we took to
be the bivouac fire of our scout Narcisse. This proved
to be the case, for on advancing we found that worthy
sitting against a tree comfortably smoking his pipe.
What would a Frenchman do without his *tabac ?*

It was good news that we need not go any farther
for an hour. So we threw ourselves down on the
ground and assailed Narcisse with questions about the
bears. We were within half a mile of the den. He
had seen the bears retire last night, and there was not
much probability of their stirring before daylight, so
we might consider them sure.

It was with considerable impatience that we waited
for the first peep of dawn. There was something exciting about this kind of work, although it was not

entirely a new experience. The Frenchmen and the Captain were old hunters; Zeno and the Professor had both taken part in a bear-hunt; while my experiences in that line were limited to sitting behind a fence half the night waiting for a bear that never came.

As soon as it was light enough to move we advanced to take up our positions.

We are now in a very pleasant valley, the rocky floor of which is entirely barren save for a few juniper bushes. In the dim morning light we can just discover that the valley is surrounded with lofty walls of rock, and is very thinly wooded with stunted spruce and cedar, while through its centre flows a narrow stream bordered with birch and poplar. At the upper end the space between the walls gradually contracts, till the valley suddenly terminates with a jagged mass of fallen rocks and *debris*, beneath which the stream appears to have its rise.

Here is the den of the wild beasts we have come to destroy. At the base of the cliff, on the left hand side, between the shattered chaos and the solid rock, arched over by the trunk of a fallen pine, there can be distinctly seen the dark opening. There is just time for a few words of instruction, and we immediately take our places. To the left there is a projection of the rock, about six feet high, fringed with juniper; a splendid position for an attack in flank. This point of vantage is assigned to the Professor and myself. On the other side are some loose boulders, forming a convenient breastwork for Zeno and Narcisse. Along the front at a distance of about fifty yards is a cluster of juniper bushes, among which lurks the Captain with his Snider; he is supported by Xavier and Nicholas, provided with potato bags, ready to rush out and secure the cubs when the old ones are killed. Our instructions were to remain perfectly quiet until the bears appeared, and then to shoot them as they came out. If silence were essential to success we certainly had it, for since arriving on the spot not a sound had been uttered, even our positions were indicated by simply a motion of the Captain's hand.

The stealthy lynx is not more noiseless in his movements than the Professor and I as we climbed to our perch and laid down on the moss, peering out through the juniper to watch that inscrutable hole. The Professor had his Remington and a good supply of cartridges; I had a double-barrelled smooth-bore, one barrel of which I had loaded with a bran new bullet, the other with buckshot. Not that I expected to kill a bear with buckshot, but it was well to have it by me in case of emergency. A good heavy charge of buckshot to fire into a bear's face might head off a rush and save some one from an ugly mauling.

We had scarcely taken our places and made a mental estimate of the distance, when out came Mr. Bruin. He came out so suddenly, and with a celerity so unusual for a bear, that I fancy he suspected something was wrong. After glancing over the valley and not discovering anything very alarming, he deliber-

ately sat down, on his own doorstep, so to speak.
And there he sat, swaying himself backward and forward in a manner peculiar to bears, indulging at the
same time in a series of the most hog-like grunts. I
observed, also, that he kept turning up his nose and
sniffing in a suspicious manner, as though he detected
something in the atmosphere not quite right.

"He ought to be dispatched before the other comes
out," whispered the Professor. "It won't do to have
them both on our hands at once." And with that he
rose to his knees.

Just then, bang! came a rattling shot from the
other side; the impulsive Zeno had opened fire.

The bear gave a snort like a frightened horse and
started to his feet, his whole body quivering with
fury. From his open throat came the most horrible
snarls and growls I have ever heard, his hot breath
making a cloud of vapor around his head through
which could be seen his glaring eye-balls. Woe be to
the unlucky mortal who now comes within range of
those deadly claws!

I glance toward the Captain; he has risen to his
feet and is taking aim. As the Snider gives voice the
bear's growling is stopped by something like a cough,
telling plainly where that ball went to.

The Professor then, to my surprise and alarm, sprang
off the rock in full view of the bear, not twenty yards
off; and there he stood, with nothing between him
and destruction but the barrel of his Remington.

Now he will have to put in a death-shot, or the bear
will be upon him before either of us can pull a trigger.

And it was a death-shot. The Remington gave a
little pop, quite insignificant compared with the two
preceding reports; but the effect upon the bear was
decisive. He collapsed all in a heap, then slowly
rolled over on his side, and lay stretched out on the
rock, only indicating by an occasional gasp and con-
vulsive movement that any life was left in him. The
whole affair had not lasted a minute, from beginning
to end; he could not have had a quicker dispatch if
he had died in the butcher's shambles.

"Look out for the she!" called the Captain. The
Professor drew back behind the rock, and we resumed
our watch upon the mouth of the den. We watched
for half an hour, but there was no further sign of life.

"What's the matter, Captain?" called Zeno; "seems
to hang fire."

"Pitch in a stone, Nimrod," was the reply.

Several stones thrown right into the den failed to
elicit any response, and we began to fear that the old
lady had given us the slip. Xavier ventured to crawl
up near enough to peep in; he even lit a quantity of
birch bark and threw it blazing into the interior, after
which, to our unutterable disgust, he pronounced it
empty. We had been all this time mounted guard
over a dead bear, while the living ones had been
making their escape.

We now gathered around and began to examine the
carcase of our prostrate quarry. He was not a very

large bear, but his hide was in very good condition for this season of the year. The question now to be decided was to whom did he belong. We had previously agreed that the hide should go to whoever gave the death-shot. But the difficulty was who gave the death-shot. The Captain's bullet had passed through the lungs, while the Professor's had pierced the brain, and either of these shots would have caused death. Zeno's aim must have been pretty well taken, for his bullet had apparently passed clear through the bear without leaving any external mark or bruise. The odds were evidently between the two shots; the Captain, however, having already several skins in his possession, generously consented to forego his claim, so it was unanimously agreed that the hide should go to the Professor.

While we were coming to this conclusion Xavier had been exploring the den, and now we were furnished with the information that the cave had a back entrance, through which the she bear and the two cubs had gone off, leaving a very distinct trail. This raised the hope that we might catch them yet, and, leaving two of the Frenchmen to skin the old fellow, the rest of us seized our guns and started in pursuit.

It is only necessary to state that we hunted those bears till sundown without the faintest gleam of success, and, after tramping till we could scarcely move a foot, scrambling through *brules* till we were as black as negroes; tumbling over rocks till we tore our clothes to tatters, and started blood at every joint; plunging through swamps till we were drenched to the skin and covered with mud, we concluded that if the bears were not enjoying themselves more than we were, they were an unhappy lot. After repeating this variety of experience till we were the most disgusted set of hunters that ever got fooled on a bear trail, we decided to adjourn the hunt *sine die*.

We had bear steaks for supper that night, cut reeking from the carcase on the spot. We did not eat them raw, by any means, but had them cooked in true hunter style; and, as that style is somewhat unique, we will describe it here in the interest of the public.

First, as the cookery book would say, you must catch your bear.

Certainly no reasonable man would expect to eat the bear's flesh while the animal was running at large; but the point we wish to emphasize is, that in order to the full enjoyment of the bear steak, it is indispensably necessary that you catch the bear yourself. Bear beef that was captured by anyone else would be pretty poor eating, and would be very likely to raise an insurrection in a third-rate-boarding-house. It is also necessary that you dine while you are still thrilling with the enthusiasm of the chase; if you wait till you have cooled down, it will require a pretty vivid imagination to convince you that all is well. Having slaughtered and skinned your bear, you next proceed to cut off your steaks—I do not remember from what part of the animal, but that is doubtless a matter of taste. My taste, under ordinary circumstances, would suggest a spot considerably to the rear of the tail.

As regards fire, you will need a good fierce one ; let it burn until there remains only a glowing heap of coals. Now, take a couple of ramrods, wipe clean, and run them through and through your thin steaks so they will be perfectly flat, then proceed to toast them over your glowing coals, taking care to turn them every few seconds so as to keep in the juices. If you are cooking for a large party, you had better press into the service as many as the fire will accommodate, and the sight of three or four fellows down on their knees around a pile of red coals, toasting slices of meat on the points of ramrods, would make quite a picture for an artist.

Now when a sufficient quantity is cooked, and there is plenty of it, the bare earth furnishes both seat and table, shanty biscuits are the only plates, pocket-knives the only cutlery, hunger the only sauce ; and, perhaps, with all these accommodations, bear steak may be found to be quite eatable.

One advantage of this style of cooking is that it does not require the lugging around of a great load of kitchen ware, hence it is admirably adapted to bivouac parties. We have cooked partridge, duck, and trout in this way, and if you only have a packet of salt among you it answers all purposes. As to bear beef as an article of diet, it may be better than starvation, but I am persuaded that if there is anything particularly delectable about it, it is owing entirely to the circumstances under which it is generally eaten. Hungry and exhausted men are ready to eat almost anything, and to eat it with considerable enthusiasm ;

but if there is anything else within easy reach, bear steaks may take a back seat for me.

After our long and fruitless chase that day, to return home that evening was out of the question; so there was no help for it but to camp down where we were. We had neither tent nor blankets, but fortunately firewood was plentiful, and we kept up a glorious blaze till near morning, while a bower of spruce boughs kept off the dews; and in that way we managed to pass the night without any more discomfort than is generally encountered in a forest bivouac. There is certainly more or less of inconvenience and privation connected with this wild bush life, and we do not recommend it to fastidious people If a man has not enough of enthusiasm in his nature to endure these things, he had better keep within reach of warm baths and feather beds and never go camping.

CHAPTER X.

"HOME, SWEET HOME."

E have thought that it would be appropriate to close this series with a chapter on the home life of the camp. Home is said to be where the heart is, and we may safely say our heart is wherever the tent is pitched.

What a delightful glamor of romance there is about the white canvas walls gleaming through the foliage or between the pine trunks.

> "Ah, me ! even now I see before me stand—
>   Among the verdant cedar boughs half hid—
>   The little radiant, airy pyramid :
> Like some wild dwelling built in fairy-land.
> Gently stirring at the quiet birth
> Of every short-lived breeze : the sunbeams greet
> The beauteous stranger in the quiet bay."

We have noticed, in camping out, that it does not take long for a home-like feeling toward the tiny dwelling to possess one, as well as quite a home-like appearance to surround a situation of this kind. Even

the lazy, languid curl of the smoke has its charms, as
it leisurely winds its way up through the pine tops.
As for the cheery sizzle of the frying-pan, as it greeted
our ears on our return from some weary excursion,
it could only be fully appreciated by the zest which
health and hunger gave us.

Ours was a jovial camp; from morning till night,
and often later, our shouts and laughter rang out,
startling the desert stillness. We had abundant
reasons for satisfaction, as we were so happily provided for in every respect. Our cook, Xavier, proved
to be a perfect genius in forest craft, and, in addition
to his abundant labors in the culinary department, he
looked after the welfare of the camp in general. He
mended everything, from a fishing-tackle to a boat.
With needle, knife, or hatchet, he was continually at
work producing something useful or necessary to the
community. The ready wit and the variety of expe-
dients he was capable of were most surprising; for
every emergency he had a resource, for every ill a
remedy; whatever might happen, Xavier was on the
qui vive; call upon him any hour of the day or night,
he was ready with the cheery response, "*Oui, monsieur,
tout bien.*" We have known few who will be remembered with greater pleasure than our active, faithful,
good-natured little Frenchman. This, perhaps, will
explain why I am able to state that we were as comfortable in camp as we could wish to be.

Now, concerning our home life. One important
consideration was to adopt some method of taking our

meals with as much comfort as possible. At first we supposed that the earth would afford very suitable tables and seats, without any further ado, and for some time took our meals reclining on the grass in various attitudes; but this method, though cheap enough, was found to have its inconveniences.

We once had the honor of enjoying the hospitality and sharing the quarters of a gentleman in the musk-rat business. The bare earth was the bed, the sky was the roof, and our own overcoat was the blanket. We had plenty of room and good ventilation, but still the accommodations were not all that could be desired. Somehow we could not sleep; we were harassed all night by a lingering suspicion that our bed had not been made up. Mentioning this circumstance to our host next morning, he remarked, "Young man, you should scrape holes to lay your bones in."

Just so with our dining-room difficulties. We had plenty to choose from, but somehow it was difficult to find places that seemed to fit us at all comfortably. We tried to compromise the matter by propping our-selves against the trees, and immediately the diffi-culty of pine gum obtruded itself. Xavier came to the rescue at last and solved the problem in a most ingenious manner. He cut a couple of logs of proper length and thickness, rolled them into position in front of the tent, and upon their upper surfaces he cut a number of circular spots, about as large as a restaurant table for one; then, by sitting astride of a log with one of these places between our knees, we were enabled ever after to take our meals in decency and comfort.

As to provisions, we managed to keep ourselves pretty well supplied. Our active fishing-lines and shotguns were useful auxiliaries of the kitchen, and we drew upon the castle for flour, biscuits, tea, potatoes and other vegetables; so that we were furnished with as good a variety as one could expect under the circumstances.

Sometimes it rained. On one occasion it rained for two whole days and nights. But our tent was waterproof and shed off all the rain that came through the pines; so we had only to remain under cover and make all snug. These were the times that tried our resources; for although our field sports were positively endless, our stock of indoor amusements was very limited. Reading was the great stand-by. We had with us a volume that has charmed away many a weary hour, the darling of our pleasure library, dear old Christopher North; with what interest and pleasure did we pore over those charming "recreations," while the rain pattered down on the roof of the tent. Those entrancing descriptions of sport and adventure seemed so appropriate to our present situation. With Christopher North in one pocket, and Sir Walter Scott in the other, we are prepared to stand a week's rain anywhere.

But we had other employments to while away the passing hour; for instance, we spent nearly the whole of one day in making torches. We trimmed a whole lot of pine knots into serviceable flambeaux, and, in addition to this, we invented a torch composed of oakum, pine gum, and birch bark. The oakum we obtained by fraying a lot of old rope, the turpentine was supplied in abundance by the surrounding pines. We discovered that oakum, well soaked in turpentine, rolled up tightly in sheets of birch bark and fastened with wire, formed really a brilliant outdoor lamp. It could be easily snuffed and trimmed by hitting it against a tree.

The unquenchable Zeno was the inventor of this "New Light," and he was so tickled with the success of the idea that he enticed me out into the woods for half a night holding one of his torches while he shot a lynx that was lurking around the camp. His theory was that the animal would be attracted by the light to within gunshot, and then he would be sure to hit it; there could be no doubt about that. We certainly had light enough to have shot a menagerie, but the lynx, apparently, had his own reasons for loving darkness rather than light. It was not very exciting work holding that torch, though the shadows leaped and danced in a manner that was confusing, to say the least of it. But when the hot turpentine began to run blazing down on to my fingers, I had excitement enough for a whole circus. Zeno hovered on the outskirts of the light, peering out into the darkness, with his finger on the trigger. It would certainly have gone hard with anyone that had ventured within reach just then; and no one knew that, apparently, better than the lynx did. I saw Zeno, at last, kneeling behind a log, with his gun at rest, taking aim at some invisible foe; and that was the last view I had of him as I shied the stump of the torch at his red head and started for home. It is still the missing lynx.

We made those torches, and a number of other useful articles, one wet day when we could not do anything else. On the whole, a wet day is long enough in camp. We have no objection to windy weather, cold weather, or any other kind of weather, if it will only admit of carrying on outdoor operations; but from wet grass, wet trees, a damp, humid atmosphere, and a drenching downpour when we are under canvas, St. Swithin defend us.

The most popular institution of the camp was the evening bonfire. Just a little way in front of the tent we built a stone "caboose," on the top of which we raised every evening a goodly pile of gummy pine; and as the curtains of night were lowered, a cheery blaze sprang up and beat back the darkness, setting our shadows dancing, bringing out the branches of the pines into strong relief and making the gloomy old forest radiant with glory.

The nights were very chilly; in fact, during the latter part of our stay they were quite frosty, so that we enjoyed the heat of the fire as much as the light. Oh! what happy times we had as the flames crackled and roared, throwing a ruddy gleam over half the lake and the adjacent islands. During the best of the blaze we generally did nothing but tend to the fire, stirring it up with long poles and heaping on the fuel, at the same time skipping around with as intense delight as a party of school-boys.

> " Amid the lurid flames our figures stand,
> As through the shrouding vapors dimly viewed ;
> To fancy seem in that strange solitude,
> Like the wild brethren of some lawless band."

As the flames gradually subsided and the fire became a glowing heap of coals, we generally settled down to enjoy it quietly.   With the fire before us, and the screen of spruce boughs behind us to keep off the wind, what glorious evenings we had, spinning campfire yarns by the hour, reading aloud from our scanty stock of literature, discussing the events of the day and the affairs of the universe generally ; occasionally filling the air and waking the echoes with jovial choruses.   What an endless variety of music we had, sacred and secular ! College choruses, Salvation Army songs, Jubilee melodies, did ever they sound so well as when we laid back and gave them mouth-room and lung-power, pealing them out with a vim that shook the very pine tops ! Our friend Zeno had a voice of most amazing compass.   It was worth going a long way to hear him sing, and to witness the glow of intense satisfaction that overspread his beaming countenance as he roared out—

> " I'm a-rolling, I'm a-rolling," etc.

Those were happy hours ; long live their memory.

Considerable interest generally centred around a big iron pot in the middle of the fire, for to the end we kept up that relic of civilization, a late supper; and as the evening wore on and the fire went down, Xavier proceeded to dish up the last meal of the day.

We have had some experiences after turning in for the night that were worth recording; some of these have been already mentioned. We had a lantern and stock of candles for indoor use; outside we used either pine knots or birch torches.

Behold us, then, with the door of the tent drawn to, the candle swinging overhead, adjusting ourselves for a few hours' sleep. Coat and boots were generally all the clothing we discarded; the boots being rolled up in the coat formed a substitute for a pillow for the most luxurious of us. Each man rolls himself in as many blankets as the temperature requires and settles himself as comfortably as possible upon the cedar twigs. A few nights of camp life will accustom one to this kind of thing, and, on the whole, we have passed as comfortable nights, and enjoyed as profound slumber, under canvas as under shingles.

When all is ready someone blows out the candle; and sometimes the candle would go out prematurely. We have known a laugh from Zeno to put out the light, when it happened to be in a line with his mouth; more than once I have been left in the darkness to struggle with blankets that would twist themselves into ropes, and get round my neck and between my legs like so many boa-constrictors. Sometimes the

candle would avenge its untimely extinction by dif-
fusing an unpleasant odor, which would draw from
the Captain the gentle request, "Nimrod, my boy,
pitch out that lantern; it smells like a soap factory
afire." And then we would gradually settle down to
repose, and the steady breathing of the party for the
rest of the night would be varied by such observations
as, "Zeno, old fellow, take your knees out of the
middle of my back, will you?" This from the Professor; or from the Captain, "Zeno, old man, for pity's
sake put your big feet outside the tent. I declare we
shall have to put you in irons if you don't behave
better than this."

If not a travelling preacher, Zeno certainly was a
travelling sleeper, for he never woke up within several
yards of where he laid down, and generally made a
circuit of the tent before morning.

There were occasional disturbances without that
sometimes broke up our repose.

One night I was enjoying a long and troubled dream,
the substance of which was that I had been sentenced
to be trampled to death by an elephant, and the sen-
tence was being carried out, when I awoke and found
Zeno crawling over me on his hands and knees, shed-
ding his blankets as he rose to his feet outside the
tent.

"What's the matter, Zeno?"

"Hush! man, keep quiet; d'ye hear that?"

"Too-whoo! too-whoo!"

We saw the point; the hoot of the night owl had

10

roused the sportsman, and he was bound to put in a shot.

We lay listening to his footsteps as he glided stealthily about seeking for that mysterious bird, whose derisive "too-whoo" sounded like the chuckle of some imp of darkness. It was not long until a report rang out with a most unmerciful crash that scared the entire camp, and a minute later Zeno inserted his head into the tent with the remark, "Say, boys, I came near hitting the biggest owl I ever saw; I declare it was as big as a turkey."

This was getting to be an old story. Zeno was always very near hitting something, except on one occasion when he came very near missing—the dog.

But it takes a pretty good shot to hit an owl in the gloom of a pine forest. Minerva's bird has a reputation for sagacity, and he is generally wise enough to keep out of the way of a shotgun.

By the way, it occurs to us that the owl is a bird whose character is very much misunderstood. For instance, we speak of the "melancholy owl." This is surely a mistake, for all the owls we have ever met had a decided vein of humor in their natures. For facetiousness and a taste for playing practical jokes on people, commend to me the jovial owl. There is something in his grave bearing and solemn expression that sharpens the edge of his grim humor, for there is no fool like the wise fool. And when the grey spectre, with its staring goggle-eyes and noiseless flight, has scared some simple rustic out of half his scanty wits does not the hoarse "too-whoo" sound like the smothered snicker of impish merriment.

Then again, we hear of the "moping owl," the "boding owl;" no such thing, the owl is the most rakish and jovial bird in the whole range of ornithology. He is, in fact, a rollicking, dissipated character; he gets on the spree every night, and never goes home till morning. The place of the owl in this department of nature requires to be better understood.

These were some of the thoughts that crossed our mind on that memorable occasion. Possibly we might have collected the material for quite a dissertation on this neglected department of ornithology had not 'sleep, balmy sleep" once more asserted her sway, and we sank into blissful unconsciousness.

> " Look through the opening in the canvas wall,
>   Through which, by fits, the scarce-felt breezes play,
>   Upon four happy souls thine eye will fall ;
>   The summer lambs are not more blest than they.
> On the green twigs all motionless they lie ;
>   In dreams romantic—dreams of balmy sleep ;
> The filmy air slow glimmering on their eye,
>   And in their ear the murmuring of the deep."

We have only to add, in closing our narrative, that we broke up camp at the end of September, and returned to town in time for the opening of college. Zeno and I entered immediately upon our studies, while the Professor went across the line and accepted a tutorship in a Southern school.

The Camping Song at the beginning of the story was composed in memory of our campaign.

BOOKS

PUBLISHED BY

WILLIAM BRIGGS,

78 & 80 KING STREET EAST,

TORONTO.

By the Rev. John Lathern, D.D.

The Macedonian Cry. A Voice from the Lands of Brahma and Buddha, Africa and Isles of the Sea, and A Plea for Missions. 12mo, cloth $0 70

The Hon. Judge Wilmot, late Lieut.-Governor of New Brunswick. A Biographical Sketch. Introduction by the Rev. D. D. Currie. With Artotype portrait. Clo., 12mo. 0 75

Baptisma. Exegetical and Controversial. Cloth, 12mo.... 0 75

By the Rev. E. Barrass, M.A.

Smiles and Tears; or, Sketches from Real Life. With Introduction by the Rev. W. H. Withrow, D.D. Bound in cloth, gilt edges, extra gilt 0 50

By the Rev. J. Cynddylan Jones.

Studies in Matthew. 12mo, cloth. (Canadian Copyright Edition) 1 25

"This is a remarkable volume of Sermons. The style, while severly logical, reminds us in its beauty and simplicity of Ruskin. These are models of what pulpit discourses ought to be."—*Methodist Recorder.*

Studies in Acts. 12mo, cloth............................ 1 50

"No exaggeration to say that Mr. Jones is fully equal to Robertson at his best, and not seldom superior to him."—*Methodist Recorder.*

Studies in Gospel of St. John. 12mo, cloth 1 50

By the Rev. J. Jackson Wray.

Honest John Stallibrass. Illustrated, 12mo, cloth $1 00

Matthew Mellowdew; A Story with More Heroes than One.
Illustrated. Cloth, $1.00. Extra gilt 1 25

> "In Matthew Mellowdew, the advantages and happiness of leading
> a Christian life are urged in an earnest and affecting style."—*Irish
> Times.*

Paul Meggit's Delusion. Illustrated. Cloth $1 00

> "A strong and heartily-written tale, conveying sound moral and
> religious lessons in an unobjectionable form."—*Graphic.*

Nestleton Magna; A Story of Yorkshire Methodism. Illustrated. Cloth 1 00

> "No one can read it without feeling better for its happy simple
> piety; full of vivacity, and racy of the genuine vernacular of the
> District."—*Watchman.*

By the Rev. W. H. Withrow, D.D., F.R.S.C

Canadian in Europe. Being Sketches of Travel in France,
Italy, Switzerland, Germany, Holland, Belguim, Great
Britain and Ireland. Illustrated. Cloth, 12mo 1 25

"Valeria," the Martyr of the Catacombs. A Tale of Early
Christian Life in Rome. Illustrated. Cloth 0 75

> "The subject is skillfully handled, and the lesson it conveys is
> noble and encouraging."—*Daily Chronicle.*
> "A vivid and realistic picture of the times of the persecution of the
> Early Christians under Diocletian."—*Watchman.*
> "The Story is fascinatingly told, and conveys a vast amount of in-
> formation."—*The Witness.*

King's Messenger; or, Lawrence Temple's Probation.
12mo, cloth 0 75

> "A capital story. . . We have seldom read a work of this kind with
> more interest, or one that we could recommend with greater con-
> fidence."—*Bible Christian Magazine.*

Neville Trueman, the Pioneer Preacher. A Tale of the.
War of 1812. 12mo, cloth. Illustrated 0 75

Methodist Worthies. Cloth, 12mo, 165 pp 0 60

Romance of Missions. Cloth, 12mo, 160 pp 0 60

Great Preachers. Ancient and Modern. Cloth, 12mo 0 60

Intemperance; Its Evils and their Remedies. Paper 0 15

Is Alcohol Food? Paper, 5c., per hundred.. . ... 3 00

Prohibition the Duty of the Hour. Paper, 5c., per hundred . 3 00

The Bible and the Temperance Question. Paper 0 10

The Liquor Traffic. Paper 0 05

The Physiological Effects of Alcohol. Paper 0 10

Popular History of Canada. 600 pp., 8vo. Eight Steel
Portraits, One Hundred Wood Cuts, and Six Coloured
Maps. Sold only by Subscription 3 00

2

By the Rev. J. S. Evans.

Christian Rewards; or, I. The Everlasting Rewards for Children Workers; II. The Antecedent Millennial Reward for Christian Martyrs. With notes:—1. True Christians may have Self-love but not Selfishness; 2. Evangelical Faith-works; 3. Justification by Faith does not include a Title to Everlasting Reward. 12mo, cloth 0 50

The One Mediator. Selections and Thoughts on the Propitiatory Sacrifice and Intercessions of our Great High-Priest. 12mo, cloth 1 00

By the Rev. Egerton Ryerson, D.D., LL.D.

Loyalists of America and Their Times. 2 Vols., large 8vo, with Portrait. Cloth, $5; half morocco $7 00

Canadian Methodism; Its Epochs and Characteristics. Handsomely bound in extra cloth, with Steel Portrait of the Author. 12mo, cloth, 440 pp 1 25

The Story of My Life. Edited by Rev. Dr. Nelles, Rev. Dr. Potts, and J. George Hodgins, Esq., LL.D. With Steel Portrait and Illustrations. (Sold only by Subscription.) Cloth, $3; sheep 4 00

By the Rev. Wm. Arthur, M.A.

Life of Gideon Ouseley. Cloth 1 00

All are Living. An attempt to Prove that the Soul while Separate from the Body is Consciously Alive. Each, 3c., per hundred 2 00

Did Christ Die for All? Each, 3c.; per hundred.......... 2 00

Free, Full, and Present Salvation. Each, 3c.; per hundred 2 00

Heroes. A Lecture delivered before the Y.M.C.A. in Exeter Hall, London. Each, 5c.; per hundred................ 3 00

Is the Bible to Lie Under a Ban in India? A Question for Christian Electors. Each, 3c.; per hundred 2 00

May we Hope for a Great Revival. Each, 3c.; per hundred. 2 00

Only Believe. Each, 3c.; per hundred 2 00

The Christian Raised to the Throne of Christ. Each, 3c.; per hundred 2 00

The Conversion of All England. Each, 3c.; per hundred.. 2 00

The Duty of Giving Away a Stated Portion of Your Income. each, 5c.; per hundred............. .... 3 00

The Friend whose Years do not Fail. Each, 3c.; per hundred 2 00

By the Rev. W. M. Punshon, D.D., LL.D.

Lectures and Sermons. Printed on thick superfine paper, 378 pp., with fine Steel Portrait, and strongly bound in extra fine cloth.. $1 00
> This volume contains some of Dr. Punshon's grandest Lectures and Sermons, which have been listened to by tens of thousands who will remember them as brilliant productions from an acknowledged genius.

Canada and its Religious Prospects. Paper............. 0 05

Memorial Sermons. Containing a Sermon, each, by Drs. Punshon, Gervase Smith, J. W. Lindsay, and A. P. Lowrey. Paper, 25c.; cloth 0 35

Tabor; or, The Class-meeting. A Plea and an Appeal. Paper, each 5c.; per dozen 0 30

The Prodigal Son, Four Discourses on. 87 pages. Paper, cover, 25c.; cloth..................................... 0 35

The Pulpit and the Pew: Their Duties to each other and to God. Two Addresses. Paper cover, 10c.; cloth. 0 45

By the Rev. E. H. Dewart, D.D.

Broken Reeds; or, The Heresies of the Plymouth Brethren. New and enlarged edition.................. 0 10

High Church Pretentions Disproved; or, Methodism and the Church of England.............................. 0 10

Living Epistles; or, Christ's Witnesses in the World. 12mo, cloth, 288 pp.................................. 1 00
> Rev. Dr. A. C. GEORGE, in the New York *Christian Advocate,* says:—"These are, without exception, admirable essays, clear, earnest, logical, convincing, practical, and powerful. They are full of valuable suggestions for ministers, teachers, class-leaders, and all others who desire to present and enforce important biblical truths."
>
> The New York *Observer* says:—"The essays are practical, earnest, and warm, such as ought to do great good, and the one on Christianity and Scepticism is very timely and well put."

Misleading Lights. A Review of Current Antinomian Theories—The Atonement and Justification, 3c.; per dozen 0 30

Songs of Life. A Collection of Original Poems. Cloth 0 75

Spurious Catholicity. A Reply to the Rev. James Roy.... 0 10

The Development of Doctrine. Lecture delivered before the Theological Union, Victoria College.............. 0 20

What is Arminianism? with a Brief Sketch of Arminius. By Rev. D. D. Whedon, D.D., LL.D., with Introduction by Dr. Dewart 0 10

Waymarks; or, Counsels and Encouragements to Penitent Seekers of Salvation, 5c.; per hundred 3 00

4

By the Rev. J. C. Seymour.

The Temperance Battlefield, and How to Gain the Day.
Illustrated. 12mo, cloth $0 65
Voices from the Throne; or, God's Call to Faith] and
Obedience. Cloth.. 0 50

By the Rev. Alex. Sutherland, D.D.

A Summer in Prairie-Land. Notes of Tour through the
North-West Territory. Paper, 40 cts.; cloth 0 70
Erring Through Wine................................... 0 05

By the Rev. George H. Cornish.

Cyclopædia of Methodism in Canada. Containing Historical,
Educational, and Statistical Information, dating from the
beginning of the work in the several Provinces in the
Dominion of Canada, with Portrait and Illustrations.
Cloth, $4.50; sheep..................................... 5 00
Pastor's Record and Pocket Ritual. Russia limp, 75 cents.
Roan, with flap and pocket 0 90

By the Rev. W. J. Hunter, D.D.

The Pleasure Dance and its Relation to Religion and
Morality.. 0 10
Popular Amusements 0 10

By John Ashworth.

Strange Tales from Humble Life. First series. 12mo, 470
pp., cloth 1 00
Strange Tales from Humble Life. Second series, cloth.... 0 45

By the Rev. H. F. Bland.

Soul-Winning. A Course of Four Lectures delivered at Victoria University 0 30
Universal Childhood Drawn to Christ. With an Appendix
containing remarks on the Rev. Dr. Burwash's "Moral
Condition of Childhood." Paper..... .... 0 10

By the Rev. John Carroll, D.D.

Case and His Contemporaries. A Biographical History of Methodism in Canada. 5 vols., cloth.................. $4 90

Father Corson; being the Life of the late Rev. Robert Corson. 12mo, cloth 0 90

"My Boy Life." Presented in a Succession of True Stories. 12mo, cloth, 300 pp................................ 1 00

Water Baptism. Paper 0 10

Exposition Expounded, Defended and Supplemented. Limp cloth.................................... 0 4?

School of the Prophets, Father McRorey's Class, and Squire Firstman's Kitchen Fire .... 0 7?

Thoughts and Conclusions of a Man of Years, Concerning Churches and Church Connection. Paper .... 0 0?

By the Rev. S. G. Phillips, M.A.

The Evangelical Denominations of the Age............. 0 15

The need of the World. With Introduction by the Rev. S. S. Nelles, D.D., LL.D. Cloth...................... 1 00

The Methodist Pulpit. A Collection of Original Sermons from Living Ministers of the United Methodist Church in Canada. Edited by the Rev. S. G. Phillips............ 1 25

By the Rev. Hugh Johnston, M.A., B.D.

Toward the Sunrise. Being Sketches of Travel in the East. Illustrated. To which is added a Memorial Sketch of Rev. W. M. Punshon, LL.D., with Portrait. 460 pp., 12mo, cloth 1 25

The Practical Test of Christianity. A Sermon delivered before the Theological Union, Victoria College, 1883 .... 0 2?

Prize Essay on Missions.

The Heathen World: Its Need of the Gospel, and the Church's Obligation to Supply It. By Rev. Geo. Patterson, D.D. Price, 12mo., cloth.................. 0 70

By the Rev. George Sexton, M.A., LL.D.

Biblical Difficulties Dispelled. Being an Answer to Queries Respecting So-Called Discrepancies in Scripture, Misunderstood and Misinterpreted Texts, etc., etc. 12mo, cloth 1 00

History's Testimony to Christ. A Discourse preached in St. Augustine's Church, Clapham, England, 1877. New and Revised Edition. Paper, net 0 20

Aldersyde. A Border Story of Seventy Years Ago. By Annie S. Swan. Illustrated, 12mo, cloth extra, 318 pp.. **$1 25**

Jock Halliday, a Grass-Market Hero; or, Sketches of Life and Character in an Old City Parish. By Robina F. Hardy. 12mo, cloth, illustrated, 192 pp **0 65**

William and Mary. A Tale of the Siege of Louisburg, 1745. By David Hickey. 12mo, cloth, 317 pp **1 00**

From Wealth to Poverty; or, The Tricks of the Traffic. A Story of the Drink Curse. By Rev. Austin Potter. 12mo, cloth. 328 pp **0 90**

The Old Vice and the New Chivalry. Ammunition for the "Scott Act Campaign." By I. Templeton-Armstrong. 12mo, cloth, 178 pp., illustrated **0 75**

The Acme Sabbath-School Reader and Reciter. This is the latest and best Sabbath-School Reader Reciter and Dialogue Book published. It contains 192 pp. of the choicest material—*all usable* **0 35**

Anecdotes of the Wesleys. By Rev. J. B. Wakeley. With Introduction by Rev. J. McClintock, D.D., LL.D. 12mo, cloth. With a Portrait. 391 pp...... .... **1 00**

Heroes of Methodism. Containing Sketches of Eminent Methodist Ministers. By Rev. J. B. Wakeley. 12mo, cloth, 470 pp... **1 00**

Counsels to Young Converts. Abridged from Dr. Wise's "Convert's Counsellor." By Rev. A. Sutherland, D.D. 18mo, cloth, 180 pp **0 30**

Wesley's Doctrinal Standards. The Sermons, Analysis and Notes. By Rev. N. Burwash, S.T.D. 8vo, cloth **2 50**

Bits from Blinkbonny; or, The Bell O' The Manse. A Tale of Scottish Village Life between 1841 and 1851. Six Original Illustrations. By John Strathesk. 12mo, cloth **1 25**

Happy Hours. A Book for the Young. With Hundreds of Pictures. 4to, boards............................... **0 60**

Wandering Lights. A Stricture on the Doctrines and Methods of Brethrenism. By Rev. R. Strachan. Paper **0 10**

The Gospel of Mark. (From Teacher's Edition of Revised New Testament.) With Marginal Passages, Etc., Etc., including Three Colored Maps of Palestine. Paper, 15c.; cloth **0 50**

Studies in Book of Mark. For Teachers, Pastors, and Parents. By Rev. D. C. Hughes, A.M. 8vo, paper, 60c.; cloth **$1 00**

The Gospel to the Poor vs. Pew Rents. By B. F. Austin, B.D. Introduction by Dr. Carman. Paper, 25c.; cloth **0 35**

Golden Wedding-Day; or, Semi-Centennial Pulpit and Pew of Richmond Street Methodist Church, Toronto. By Rev. Isaac Tovell, M.A. Paper **0 25**

Immersion. Proved to be not a Scriptural Mode of Baptism but a Romish Invention, etc. By Rev. W. A. McKay, B.A. With Appendix—"A Reviewer Reviewed." Paper, 25c.; cloth.. $0 50

Two Fundamental Errors in the Teaching of Plymouth Brethren. By Rev. T. G. Williams. Each 2c.; per doz. 0 20

Why I am a Methodist. Paper, 2c.; per doz 0 20

A Wesleyan Methodist's Thoughts—About Prayer, the Bible, Baptism, The Covenant, The Lord's Supper, etc., etc. Paper 0 05

Renewing the Covenant. Each 5c.; per 100.............. 3 00

Advice to One who Meets in Class. By Rev. Robert Newstead. Each 3c.; per doz 0 30

Relation of Children to the Fall, the Atonement, and the Church. By N. Burwash, S.T.D. Paper 0 15

Scripture Baptism. Per 100 .... 0 50

Rules of Society. Per 100 .... 0 50

    With Scripture Proofs. Per 100.................... 1 50

    With Trial Ticket Combined. Per 100 .... 1 00

Church Class-Books. With Pocket for Tickets 0 20

Model Deed Blanks. For Church Property. Per Set of Two 0 20

Permits to Sell Church Property—Blanks. Per Set of Two 0 10

Declaration to Fill Vacancies on Trustee Boards. Per Set of Two.. 0 10

Declaration to Increase Number of Trustees. Per Set of Two.. 0 10

Model Deed Act. Containing Statutes of Canada, also Statutes of Ontario, Respecting the Methodist Church. Paper 0 25

Discipline. Cloth, 60c.; limp French morrocco............ 1 00

Lectures and Sermons delivered before the Theological Union of Victoria College.

Members One of Another. Sermon by Rev. Dr. Nelles ....⎫
The Genesis, Nature, and Results of Sin. Lecture by Rev. ⎬0 20
    N. Burwash, S.T.D. Paper ....⎭

The Development of Doctrine. Lecture by Rev. E. H. Dewart, D.D................................... ⎫
⎬0 20
The Work of Christ. Sermon by Rev. E. A. Stafford. Paper ⎭

The Cherubim. Lecture by Rev. W. Jeffers, D.D ....⎫
The Ordering of Human Life. Sermon by Rev. W. W. ⎬0 20
    Ross. Paper ....⎭

The Obligations of Theology to Science. Lecture by Rev.
A. Burns, D.D., LL.D., ... } 0 20
The Divine Call to the Ministry. Sermon by Rev. E. B.
Ryckman, D.D. Paper ....

Certainties in Religion. Lecture by Rev. J. A. Williams, D.D.
The Soul's Anchor. Sermon by Rev. George McRitchie.
Paper .... } 0 20

Sin and Grace. Lecture by Rev. James Graham ....
The Practical Test of Christianity. Sermon by Rev. Hugh
Johnston, M.A., B.D. Paper .... } 0 20

Eternal Punishment. Lecture by Rev. W. I. Shaw, M.A.,
LL.B ....
The Coming One. Sermon by Rev. W. R. Parker, M.A.
Paper .... } 0 20

Lectures and Sermons. From 1879 to 1882. In One
Volume. Cloth 0 75

———

The Life of "Chinese" Gordon, R.E., C.B. With Portrait
on the title-page. By Charles H. Allen, F.R.G.S.,
Secretary of British and Foreign Anti-Slavery Society.
Post-free.. 0 05

"A GREAT BOOK."

The Natural Law in the Spiritual World. By Henry
Drummond, F.R.C.E., F.G.S. 414 pp. New Edition
Ready...................................... 1 75

"This is every way a remarkable work, worthy of the thoughtful
study of all who are interested in the great question now pending
as to the relations of natural science to revealed religion. . . A
mine of practical and suggestive illustrations."—*Living Church.*

Father Lambert's Notes on Ingersoll. Paper, 20c.; cloth 0 50

"It is a masterly refutation of Ingersoll. It should be widely cir-
culated."—Rev. T. G. WILLIAMS, President Montreal Conference.

Aggressive Christianity. 12mo, cloth, 60 cts; paper 0 35
Godliness. By Mrs. Catharine Booth. With Introduction
by Daniel Steele, D.D. 12mo, cloth, 60c.; paper 0 35

———

Applied Logic. By the Rev. S. S. Nelles, LL.D. Cloth.. 0 75
Arrows in the Heart of the King's Enemies; or Atheistic
Errors of the Day Refuted, and the Doctrine of a Personal
God Vindicated. By the Rev. Alexander W. McLeod, D.D.
formerly editor of the *Wesleyan*, Halifax, N.S., 12mo,
cloth 0 45

Burial in Baptism. A Colloquy, in which the Claims of Ritual Baptism in Romans vi. 3, 4, Colossians ii. 12 are examined and Shown to be Visionary. By the Rev. T. L. Wilkinson. Paper, 5c.; per hundred.................... **$3 00**

Catechism of Baptism. By the Rev. D. D. Currie. Cloth. **0 50**

Certainties of Religion. By the Rev. J. A. Williams, D.D., F.T.L., and The Soul's Anchor. By the Rev. George McRitchie **0 20**

Christian Perfection. By the Rev. J. Wesley. Paper, 10c.; cloth **0 20**

Church Membership; or, The Conditions of New Testament and Methodist Church Membership Examined and Compared. By the Rev. S. Bond, Methodist Minister of the Montreal Conference. 18mo, cloth, 72 pp. **0 35**

Circuit Register. **1 50**

Class-Leader, The; His Work and How to Do it. By J. Atkinson, M.A. Cloth, 12mo, cheap edition **0 60**

> "It is practical, sprightly, devout, and full of profit. We would urge every class-leader to possess himself of a copy."—*Christian Guardian.*

Class-Meeting, The. Its Spiritual Authority and Practical Value. By the Rev. J. A. Chapman, M.A **0 10**

Conversations on Baptism. By the Rev. Alexander Langford. Cloth **0 30**

Companion to the Revised New Testament. By Alexander Roberts, D.D., and an American Reviser. Paper, 30c.; cloth **0 65**

The Life of Alexander Duff, D.D., LL.D. By George Smith, C.J.E., LL.D., Author of "The Life of John Wilson, D.D., F.R.S.," Fellow of the Royal Geographical and Statistical Society, &c., with an Introduction by Wm. M. Taylor, D.D. Two large octavo volumes, bound in cloth, with Portraits by Jeens **3 00**

Journal of the General Conference, for the years 1874, 1878, and 1882. Paper, 60c.; cloth **0 75**

Journal of First United General Conference, 1883. Paper, 70c.; cloth **1 00**

Lectures and Sermons. Delivered before the "Theological Union" of the University of Victoria College. 1879 to 1882 inclusive, in one volume, cloth.................. **0 75**

The above may be had separately, in paper covers, each.. **0 20**

Librarian's Account Book **0 50**

Life and Times of Anson Green, D.D. Written by himself. 12mo, cloth, with Portrait...................... **1 00**

Lone Land Lights. By the Rev. J. McLean. Cloth **0 30**

Memories of James B. Morrow. By the Rev. A. W. Nicholson. Cloth **0 75**

Memorials of Mr. and Mrs. Jackson. With Steel Portrait.
Cloth $0 35

Methodist Catechisms. No. 1., per dozen, 25c.; No. II., per
dozen, 60c.; No III., per dozen, 75c. Three in one.
Cloth. Each 0 25

Methodist Hymn-Books. In various sizes and styles of
binding. Prices from 30 cents upwards.

Old Christianity against Papal Novelties. By Gideon
Ouseley, Illustrated. Cloth............................. 1 00

Prayer and its Remarkable Answers. By W. W. Patton,
D.D. Cloth.. 1 00

Recreations. A Book of Poems. By the Rev. E. A. Stafford,
M.A., President of the Montreal Conference. It is beauti-
fully printed on English paper, and bound in extra English
cloth, bevelled edges, and lettered in gold.............. 0 35

Religion of Life; or, Christ and Nicodemus. By John G.
Manly. Cloth... 0 50

"Of the orthodox evangelical type, vigorous and earnest. Most
great theological questions come up for more or less of notice, and
Mr. Manly's remarks are always thoughtful and penetrating."—*The
British Quarterly Review.*

Roll Book. Designed for the Use of Infant Classes. One-
quire Book containing lines for 178 Scholars, and lasting
for 13 years, $1.00; and a Two-quire Book similar to
above 1 50

Secretary's Minute Book. New design. By Thomas Wallis.
Boards 0 60

Secretary's Minute Book 0 50

Sermons on Christian Life. By the Rev. C. W. Hawkins.
Cloth 1 00

Spiritual Struggles of a Roman Catholic. An Autobio-
graphical Sketch. By the Rev. Louis N. Beaudry.
Steel Portrait. Cloth 1 00

"We do not remember having seen a volume better fitted than this
for universal circulation among Protestants and Romanists."—
Talmage's Christian at Work.

Sunday-School Class Book. Cloth, per dozen 0 75

Sunday-School Class Book. New design. Cloth, per doz . 1 50

Sunday-School Register 0 50

Sunday-School Record (new) for Secretaries 1 25

Theological Compend. By the Rev. Amos Binney. 32mo,
cloth 0 30

The Guiding Angel. By Kate Murray. 18mo, cloth 0 30

Weekly Offering Book.. 1 50

Within the Vail; or, Entire Sanctification. By the Rev.
James Caswell 0 10

☞ *Any Book mailed post-free on receipt of price.*

1

USEFUL BOOKS.

Webster's Unabridged Dictionary, with Supplement. Bound
in sheep $12 50

Webster's Unabridged Dictionary, with Supplement and
Denison's Index. Bound in sheep 13 50

Worcester's Unabridged Dictionary, with Supplement.
Full sheep 11 00

Chambers's Encyclopædia. 10 vols., cloth 25 00
     "   "   10 vols., half morocco, extra.. 50 00

Schaff-Herzog Encyclopædia. 3 vols., cloth 18 00
     "   "   3 vols., sheep 22 50
     "   "   3 vols., half morocco 27 00

Smith's Bible Dictionary. 4 vols., cloth 20 00
     "   "   "   4 vols., sheep................ 25 00

Smith & Barnum's Bible Dictionary. 8vo, cloth........ 5 00

**McClintock & Strong's Biblical, Theological, and
Ecclesiastical Cyclopædia.**
         10 vols., cloth 50 00
         10 vols., sheep 60 00
         10 vols., half morocco 80 00

Kitto's Biblical Cyclopædia. 3 vols., cloth 12 60

Young's Great Concordance. Cloth 5 00
     "   "   "   Half Russia, net 5 75

Matthew Henry's Commentary. 3 vols., cloth, net 12 00
     "   "   9 vols., cloth, net 15 00

Adam Clarke's Commentary. Latest edition. Edited by
Thornley Smith.
         6 vols., cloth......................... 20 00
         6 vols., sheep 24 00
         6 vols., half morocco 30 00

Adam Clarke's Commentary. Edited by Dr. Curry. Cloth,
per vol. 3 00

&c.,   &c.,   &c.,   &c.

All the latest English and American editions of standard and
other books kept in stock or got to order promptly. Sunday-school
Library and Prize Books in great variety.

WILLIAM BRIGGS,
78 & 80 KING STREET EAST, TORONTO.

C. W. COATES, MONTREAL.   S. F. HUESTIS, HALIFAX, N.S.

VALUABLE WORKS,

BY

Rev. J. CYNDDYLAN JONES,

And other eminent authors.

Crown 8vo, cloth boards, Second Edition, price $1.50.

STUDIES IN THE ACTS OF THE APOSTLES.
By the Rev. J. CYNDDYLAN JONES.

THE BISHOP OF LIVERPOOL says :—" It is a book of great freshness, vigour, and originality, as well as thoroughly sound in doctrine, and I wish it a wide circulation."

THE DEAN OF PETERBOROUGH :—"It is full of interest, and very fresh and suggestive. You have conferred a real benefit upon the Church, and I hope you will be encouraged to give us some more commentaries in the same strain. They will be valuable."

Opinions of the Press.

"Full of fresh thoughts, strikingly put. . . . Models of what sermons should be. . . . Intellectual stimulus to the most cultured reader. . . . All will repay reading, not only once, but a second, and even a third time."—*The Christian World.*

"A very suggestive volume. . . . A fresh and vigorous treatment. . . . Singular ability. . . . The idea an excellent one, and could not have been better carried out."—*The Literary World.*

"This is in every way a noteworthy and most striking book. . . . We have seldom read sermons out of which so many capital, terse, aphoristic sentences could be picked. . . . Freshness and force. . . . Good, nervous, homely, expressive English, and without a needless word. . . . Readers of this book will find a great many things which have perhaps never struck them before, but which are very natural, simple, and beautiful. . . . No one who reads this book with attention, and with an honest and earnest heart, can fail to benefit by it. It will convey numberless valuable hints to students and young preachers, and is a model of the simple, manly, earnest style most needed in the pulpit."
—*The Watchman and Wesleyan Advertiser.*

" Mr. Jones has a well-trained faculty of looking all round his subject, and of looking straight into it. He is often very suggestive, and always very methodical. Of fruitful mind and careful habit of thought, he treats no subject without putting some greater or smaller truth into a new light."—*Nonconformist.*

" The sermons possess great force and freshness. As far as we can see, there is no monotony in them—a very rare thing in sermon literature. Their spirit is as fresh and bracing as a May morning on the mountain top. Everywhere we discern a manly robustness, a boldness of conception, and a vigorous common sense. Old truths are often so quaintly and forcefully put, that they sparkle with new light, and remind us of diamonds reset."—*The Bible Christian Magazine.*

" It is pleasing to meet with such freshness and originality. . . . The fruit of extensive reading and careful thought. . . . He treats his subjects in a simple but masterly style, and he invests his themes with interest and attraction. . . . We heartily commend them to young ministers as models of simplicity, eloquence, and clearness of sty e. . . . One of the most eloquent preachers of Wales."—*South Wales Daily News.*

" The ripe fruit of a man of genius."—(*Addfed ffrwyth meddwl athrylithgar wedi cyrhaedd ei lawn dwf.*)—*Y Goleuad.*

" Admirable sermons. The style of treatment is popular and vigorous, many old points being brought out with considerable force, and many new ones revealed in a pleasing manner, by the ingenious and discerning author. . . . A store of sound thought and striking language."—*The Christian.*

" Freshness and vigour. . . . The execution is really good."—*The Freeman.*

" Signal ability. The author thinks for himself; strikes out into his own paths, and walks alone with an independent step; he does not lean on the arm of any one. We rejoice to know, from this volume, that Cambria has still preachers of original thought, fervid enthusiasm, and stirring eloquence."—*The Homilist.*

Crown 8vo, cloth boards, price $1.25.

STUDIES IN THE GOSPEL BY ST. MATTHEW.
By the Rev. J. CYNDDYLAN JONES.

Opinions of the Press.

" This is a remarkable volume of sermons in a singularly unpretending form. We never remember to have met with so much culture, freshness, power, pathos, and fire in so small a space. It is a book to be read and re-read, with new instruction and stimulus on each perusal. It is no exaggeration to say that Mr. Jones is fully equal to Robertson at his best, and not seldom superior to him in intellectual grasp, depth of thought, clearness of exposition, pointedness of appeal, and fidelity to evangelical truth. The style, which is severely logical, reminds us in its beauty and simplicity of Ruskin. These are models of what pulpit discourses ought to be. We shall look for more from the same able pen." —*Methodist Recorder.*

" Since reading Robertson's sermons in 1857 . . . . we have not derived so much pleasure and instruction as from this volume. We have read the book over and over again, and every time with additional pleasure by finding something new that had not presented itself to us before. Every sermon is full of thoughts pregnant with others. The whole sermon grows naturally out of the text, touch after touch, into a perfect whole—a thing of beauty suggestive of profounder meaning in Scripture and new lines of treatment. The author is perfectly natural, often humorous, never dull. . . . We never more heartily, nor with greater confidence, recommended a volume of sermons to the notice of our readers. Preachers who wish to learn how great thoughts can be wedded to language clear and easy, or how a sermon may be made to grow out of Scripture and not forced upon it, will do well to study Mr. Jones' style."—*Western Mail.*

"These volumes ('Studies in St. Matthew and 'Studies in the Acts') are the works of an artist who wields a literary pencil that might be envied by the best writers of modern times; and some of the passages remind us of Ruskin at his very best. 'Beauty adorning Truth' is the motto we would select to describe these works. Ripe culture, keen insight, and intense enthusiasm are their prominent characteristics. We have never met with so much thought, originality, and suggestiveness, allied with such exquisite taste, in so small a compass."—*The Essex Telegraph.*

"Seventeen of the leading topics of the first Gospel are, in this volume, made the basis of thoughtful, suggestive, well-arranged, and clearly-expressed sermons. Mr. Jones has the faculty for the effective treatment of large breadths of Scripture, seizing their salient ideas, treating them in a broad and fundamental manner, and so carrying his readers to the heart of Christianity and of life, in a way that secures attractive freshness and mind-compelling force. We welcome these 'Studies,' and shall be glad to introduce to our readers other works from the same able and glowing pen."—*General Baptist Magazine.*

"We have read these sermons with unusual gratification. They are perfectly evangelical, vigorous, and often original in thought, robust in sentiment, vivid in illustration, with frequent quaintness of expression which give piquancy to their teaching, and keep the interest of the reader wide awake."—*Baptist Magazine.*

"These sermons are really 'Studies.' They handle vital subjects with great clearness, breadth, and power. Mr. Jones is a teacher who has a right to be heard beyond the limited sphere of the pulpit. Every page of his work manifests careful thinking, clean-cut exegesis, and fine flashes of spiritual perception. While fresh in thought and happy in expression, the discourses are eminently evangelical. Christian ministers will find much to stimulate thought and quicken enthusiasm in these pages; they will also see how to redeem the pulpit from trite thinking and slipshod expression."—*Irish Congregational Magazine.*

"We regard the discourses in this volume as models of exposition; and ministers who are engaged in taking their hearers through the first Gospel cannot do better than get Mr. Jones' volume."—*Christian World Pulpit.*

"Mr. Jones writes with much literary finish and skill, and with an evident avoidance of the coarse sensationalism so common in works of the kind, for which we know not how to be sufficiently grateful."—*Christian Globe.*

"This is no ordinary book by no ordinary man. . . . It bristles from beginning to end with terse, fresh, vigorous thoughts. . . . A book which might be one of the classics of the English language."—*The Preacher's Analyst.*

MINISTERS WORKERS TOGETHER with GOD,

AND OTHER SERMONS. By F. W. BOURNE. Crown 8vo, 320 pp. Cloth boards, bevelled edges, $1.25.

"The thought is fresh and vigorous, and the spirit evangelical and earnest."—*Dickinson's Theological Quarterly*.

"Full of felicities. . . . Fine broad views. . . . Lit up with an eloquence that never flags."—*Dr. James Morison*.

*** The first Sermon in the volume has had a very large circulation in a separate form, a cheap edition of which is still on sale at 2d.

ON THE KING'S BUSINESS. By the Rev. J. O.

KEEN, D.D. Third Edition is now ready, crown 8vo, cloth boards, 70c

"Sermons are not usually very readable, but we must in all honesty make an exception of these. . . . They are in the . . . widest sense Christian. . . . There is nothing of monotony in these discourses."—*South Wales Daily News*.

Just Published. Price 70c.

SUGGESTIVE THOUGHTS FOR BUSY WORKERS.

By the same Author. Crown 8vo, cloth boards.

"Fitted to afford considerable valuable help. It is marked by . . . great intellectual vigour, incisiveness of thought, force and precision of expression, short, terse sentences, constant 'go' in the march of thought, and soundness of exposition."—*Literary World*.

THE KING'S SON ; or, A Memoir of BILLY BRAY.

By F. W. BOURNE. Twentv-second Edition. Cloth boards, 35c.

*** Her Majesty the Queen has graciously accepted a copy of this work, and expressed herself as much pleased with it.

"We are exceedingly glad to see a new and illustrated edition. . . . Some of his (Billy's) best sayings are better than Rowland Hill's, their provincialism giving to them an added charm. It is impossible to read this life without both amusement and admiration."—*Noncon-formist*.

"Admirably suited for a gift-book."—*Wesleyan Methodist Magazine*.

ALL FOR CHRIST—CHRIST FOR ALL: Illus-

trated by the Life and Labours of William M. Bailey. By F. W. BOURNE. Cloth boards, 35c.

"A better book of the kind than this we have seldom if ever fallen in with. It is packed full of soul-stirring facts, and is all aglow with holy feeling.

www.ingramcontent.com/pod-product-compliance
Lightning Source LLC
Chambersburg PA
CBHW021123020726
47500CB00003B/890